"Bex," a harsh whisper sounded. "Move. Now."

Bex's eyes flew open. Impossibly, Max stood towering over her, ski-mask guy limply hanging over his shoulder, his arms dangling toward the ground. Max jerked his head, motioning for her to run straight ahead to the aisle directly in front of them.

Stunned that she was alive and could run, she ducked and darted from the alcove, then stopped just past the endcap and looked behind her.

He yanked out his pistol and shoved it toward her. "Remember how to use one of these?" he whispered.

She swallowed, then nodded. "I haven't fired one in years."

Something dark passed in his eyes, and she knew he was remembering one of the many times he'd taken her to target practice so long ago.

And seeing him now, so calm and focused, she knew that if anyone could save her, it was Max.

But who would save her from him?

SECRET STALKER

———

LENA DIAZ

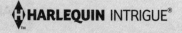
HARLEQUIN INTRIGUE®

Thank you to my editor, Allison Lyons,
and my agent, Nalini Akolekar.

This one's for George. Because he reads every book I write,
and pretends to love romance novels, all to make me happy.
Best. Husband. Ever. I love you, babe.

ISBN-13: 978-0-373-75666-7

Secret Stalker

Copyright © 2017 by Lena Diaz

Recycling programs
for this product may
not exist in your area.

Printed in U.S.A.

™ www.Harlequin.com

Lena Diaz was born in Kentucky and has also lived in California, Louisiana and Florida, where she now resides with her husband and two children. Before becoming a romantic suspense author, she was a computer programmer. A former Romance Writers of America Golden Heart® Award finalist, she has also won the prestigious Daphne du Maurier Award for Excellence in mystery and suspense. To get the latest news about Lena, please visit her website, lenadiaz.com.

Books by Lena Diaz

Harlequin Intrigue

Tennessee SWAT

Mountain Witness
Secret Stalker

Marshland Justice

Missing in the Glades
Arresting Developments
Deep Cover Detective
Hostage Negotiation

The Marshal's Witness
Explosive Attraction
Undercover Twin
Tennessee Takedown
The Bodyguard

CAST OF CHARACTERS

Max Remington—Full-time detective, part-time SWAT officer, he must put aside his hurt and anger to save the life of the woman who dumped him. But is she a murderer?

Bexley (Bex) Kane—Forced to return to her hometown, she must face the painful secrets of her past and win her former lover's trust and forgiveness before it's too late for them both.

Marcia Knolls—She blames Bex for killing her boyfriend and is obsessed with revenge. But is murder part of her plan?

Deacon Caldwell—He had everything to gain from his older brother's death years ago. But with Bex stirring up the secrets of both of their pasts, does he see her as a threat to be eliminated?

Robert Caldwell—With only months to live, has he decided to use his fortune to buy the justice he feels was denied when his oldest son was murdered?

Reggie Oliver—Impatient with her minimum-wage job, she's ready to use her upbringing as the daughter of a master criminal to get some quick cash, no matter who it hurts.

Chief Thornton—An unsolved decade-old murder case is once again his primary focus. And this time, he's going to solve it, no matter what.

Colby Vale—SWAT officer and detective, he's stuck in the middle between the chief's desire to solve his case and Max's need to protect the woman who may well be a murderer.

Chapter One

The whispers started thirty seconds after Bexley Kane walked down aisle three in the Piggly Wiggly on Magnolia Street. Not that there was a Piggly Wiggly on any other street in the tiny town of Destiny, Tennessee. With a population the size of a large high school in other parts of the state, this town could only support one grocery store. And one movie theater. And one Waffle House. But, oddly enough, there were four Starbucks. Too bad not one of them was anywhere close to Magnolia Street. Bex sure could use a venti caramel macchiato right now.

Head high, shoulders back, she began filling her cart as quickly as possible while pretending not to notice the other shoppers talking behind their hands as she passed. But, come on, did they really believe that she didn't know they were gossiping about her? She could well imagine what they were saying.

Is that who I think it is? What's it been, ten years? Why is she back in town?

You didn't hear? Her mama done passed away. I heard she died of a broken heart, on account of her daughter didn't visit even once after she got run out of town.

You think Chief Thornton will arrest her this time?

Is there a statute of limitations on murder?

"Miss Kane, nice to see you today." Mr. Dawson gave Bex a genuine, welcoming smile from behind the deli counter. "I was hoping I'd see your lovely face at least one more time before you left Destiny. You here for lunch? We've got a brand-new batch of pickled pigs' feet." He proudly thumped a large jar on top of the display case that looked like a science experiment gone horribly wrong.

Bex very nearly lost her breakfast. She averted her gaze from the nauseating sight and smiled at one of the few people in Destiny who hadn't treated her like a pariah in the week that she'd been back.

"Hello, Mr. Dawson. I called in an order for some lunch meats and grilled chicken. Could you see whether it's ready, please?"

"Gladys must have taken that order. I'll check the cooler. Won't take but a minute." He opened the massive walk-in refrigerator behind him and headed inside.

Bex checked her grocery list. The only thing left to get was mustard, one of several things she'd forgotten the first time she'd been in the store. After today's shopping trip, she should have enough to tide her over for several more days, until she finished taking care of all of the details of her mother's estate. Then she could hop into her car and leave Destiny in the dust. Again. And this time, she'd never come back.

If she remembered correctly, Mr. Dawson kept the condiments across the aisle from the meat case. Since little else had changed in this town, she doubted that had, either. She turned around—and locked gazes with the one person she'd hoped to avoid.

Max Remington.

His golden-brown eyes stared at her in shock for all of three seconds. Then they filled with anger. His jaw clamped tight and, without a word, he circled around her and headed to the sandwich counter at the other end of the deli.

Gladys miraculously appeared as if from thin air, eager to take Max's order. Bex couldn't help noticing that he was all smiles and *yes, ma'am*s, *no, ma'am*s when speaking to the older woman. But he couldn't even spare a hello for his former lover.

His curt dismissal shouldn't hurt. After all, she was the one who'd left him. But he'd been her first love. And she'd built him up in her mind over the years as her handsome hero, dreaming of what life could have been, should have been, if she'd said yes that night.

And if Bobby Caldwell hadn't died.

She grabbed a jar of mustard and allowed herself the guilty pleasure of admiring Max from beneath her lashes—all six feet two of him. At eighteen, he'd been the cutest, sweetest, most popular boy at Destiny High. At twenty-eight, he was a devastatingly handsome man with bulging biceps and muscular thighs filling out the gangly frame of his youth. His dark hair was short on the sides, thick and wavy on top. He'd been clean shaven when she'd been with him. Now his angular face was framed by neatly trimmed stubble, as if he was considering growing a beard but hadn't yet committed.

He dressed pretty much the same as he had back then: nothing fancy, just a no-nonsense button-up blue linen shirt neatly tucked into a pair of crisp jeans. In deference to the chilly autumn air outside, he wore a lightweight navy blue jacket. And as he turned to point to something in the display case for Gladys, the white lettering on his back reassured Bex that she'd made the right decision all those years ago—the letters spelled Destiny Police Department.

Good for you, Max. You chased your dream after all.

"Will you be needing anything else, Miss Kane?"

She forced her gaze away from Max, her face flushing with heat when Mr. Dawson glanced down the counter, then back at her, obviously noting her interest in her former high school sweetheart.

He handed her a brown paper sack that was stapled closed. "Your order's inside. Just show the cashier that code on the bag at checkout and she'll ring up the manager's special. That'll save you a couple of dollars."

"Thank you." She lowered her voice. "I really appreciate how nice you've been to me. You're one of the few people who's made this trip bearable."

"You don't need to thank me for doing what's right. It's a downright shame how nasty folks can be. They ought not to be throwing stones without taking a long, hard look at themselves first."

She smiled again, painfully aware that Max and Gladys had stopped talking the moment she'd thanked Mr. Dawson. Was Max looking at her? Had he decided to acknowledge her existence after all?

The sound of his boots echoed on the tile floor as he strode toward her. She clutched the bag and jar of mustard against her chest, frozen in place while she desperately tried to think of something, anything, to say.

He stalked past without even looking at her.

Bex's breath rushed out of her, deflating her like a popped balloon.

Someone cleared their throat. Mr. Dawson. He was watching her with a sympathetic expression on his face. Beside him, Gladys looked decidedly less friendly, a frown wrinkling her brow, her hands on her generous hips. There was no doubt about whose side she was on. Not that there were any sides to take. A fight required two people, and Max hadn't cared enough about the outcome to even stick around for the first volley.

Bex nodded her thanks to Mr. Dawson before putting her items in the cart and heading toward the back of the store, as if there was something else she needed. What she *really* needed was a moment to compose herself.

Not wanting to risk another encounter with Max, she strolled along the rear aisle toward the other side of the store, putting off checking out until she was certain he'd be gone.

Maybe she should just get in her RAV4 and hit the road right now. She could hire someone else to pack up her mom's house. Settling the last legal details of the estate through the mail instead of working with her lawyer in person would delay things. But at least she wouldn't have to endure one more person's disapproving stare. And her heart wouldn't have to face Max again.

She tried to convince herself that it wasn't cowardice that had her wanting to run—it was self-preservation. Because it had taken years to tape and glue the pieces of her broken heart back together. But shattering it again had only taken one angry look from Max Remington.

MAX SHUFFLED IMPATIENTLY in line behind Mable Humphries. It was the express lane, ten items or less. But she had thirty items. And the only other register that was open had three customers waiting with overflowing carts.

He blew out a frustrated breath, then forced a smile when the elderly woman looked at him.

"How are you today, Mrs. Humphries?" he asked.

"You sure are sweet to ask, Detective Remington. My joints have been aching something fierce today, and not just from the chill outside. I think we're in for a storm soon. Don't you?"

He gave her a noncommittal answer and she prattled on about her aches and pains. He wished he could just ignore her outright or tell her to hurry up. But the manners his mother and father had drilled into him couldn't be ignored.

Except, apparently, where Bexley Kane was concerned.

A twinge of guilt shot through him over the way he'd treated her. Or, rather, *ignored* her.

Destiny was too small for him not to have heard the rumors. He knew she was back in town because of her mother's recent passing. But he hadn't been prepared for actually coming face-to-face with her after all these years. He'd just… reacted. All the lines he'd rehearsed in case he ever saw her again had disappeared in a fog of rage and hurt. So he'd done the only thing he could safely do. He'd kept his mouth shut.

As Mrs. Humphries droned on, Max nodded in the appropriate places but otherwise tuned her out.

Bex. It was hard to believe that she was really here. Was she staying? Permanently? Based on her comments to Mr. Dawson about him making her "trip" bearable, Max didn't think so. Maybe he should have paid more attention to the gossip swirling around town about her instead of taking pains to avoid it every time her name came up. Then maybe he'd know what Bex's plans were so he could take the necessary precautions to ensure that he didn't run into her again.

He'd already done his duty by Bex's mom, the

sweet woman whom he and half the town had expected would become his mother-in-law one day. He'd gone to the memorial service her church had put together, a service without a casket or even an urn since her body had been shipped out of town to be interred somewhere else. As far as he knew, Bex hadn't bothered to go to the church. For his part, he'd arrived early and left fast, just in case she did show.

His mourning was done in private, when he'd planted some white lilies in Mrs. Kane's garden as a tribute to her. They'd always been her favorite, and he'd planted a new lily in her yard every Mother's Day for the past ten years.

"It sure was nice running into you, Detective." Mable's gnarled hand gripped his with surprising strength. "Hope to see you at the town picnic next weekend. I'm making some of my famous sweet potato pie."

"I wouldn't miss it, ma'am." He gently extricated his hand and returned her wave as she pushed her cart to the exit.

The young brunette at the cash register scanned Max's sandwich and handed it back to him.

"You want to make that a meal deal with chips and a drink? I can have someone run to the deli and—"

"Just the sandwich, thanks." He quickly paid and let out a breath of relief that he was finally about to get out of purgatory. He wasn't even hungry anymore. All he wanted to do was return to the police station, immerse himself in work and try to forget all about Bexley Kane.

"Everybody do what we say and no one gets hurt!"

Max jerked his head toward the entrance. Five masked gunmen with assault rifles had just run in through the front door and were pointing their guns toward the handful of customers at the other register.

The cashier beside him started screaming. One of the gunmen swung his rifle her way. Max dived over the counter, pulling the girl to the floor seconds before the countertop above them exploded in a hail of gunfire.

Chapter Two

Bex flattened herself against a cereal box endcap, pressing both of her hands against her mouth to keep from crying out.

Rat-a-tat-tat-tat-tat-tat!

Bam! Bam!

She dropped to the floor, her breaths coming out in short pants. What in the world was happening? Who would fire guns inside a Piggly Wiggly? The answer, of course, was obvious. Someone was holding up the place. But she still couldn't believe it was happening. Not here. Not in the tiny town of Destiny.

Thank God Max had plenty of time to have left before the gunman or gunmen had shown up.

And wasn't that a crazy thought, being glad the police officer was out of harm's way when he was the one person who might have been able to help her and any others trapped inside?

A scream sounded from the front of the store.

Someone else shouted. Footsteps pounded down an aisle not too far from where Bex lay on the floor. If someone was holding up the store, wouldn't they have forced the manager to open the safe in the front office? They wouldn't be running down aisles and still shooting minutes later, would they?

Bam! Bam!

That sounded like a pistol.

Rat-a-tat-tat-tat.

Automatic gunfire.

She pressed a hand to her throat. Was that a gunfight? Whoever had the pistol was at a serious disadvantage.

Another shout sounded. More footsteps.

Bam!

"Where is she?" a man yelled. "She wasn't with the ones who locked themselves in the cooler."

"How the hell should I know? Reggie said she was ready to check out. She should have been up front when we got here."

"Find her. And find that stupid cop. He's screwing everything up and I'm gonna blow his brains out."

Oh, no. Please, God, don't be talking about Max.

But in her gut, she knew they were. He was the only policeman she'd seen in the store just a few minutes before the gunmen came in. No one else could have gotten here this fast. He either hadn't left when she'd thought he had, or he'd run back into the store when he saw the gunmen go inside.

Footsteps sounded again, much closer this time. If they turned down the back aisle that ran the width of the store, they'd see her. She had to move, hide. Or better yet, find Max and get them both out of the store.

Right, like she was GI Jane or something. The only danger she faced on a typical day was whether she might get a splinter in her finger from one of the pieces of furniture that she sold at her antique store.

Move, Bex. Hurry!

She sent up a quick, silent prayer then pulled herself forward in an army crawl.

MAX CROUCHED DOWN, his pistol out in front of him while he whispered into his cell phone and made his way down aisle five toward the front of the store again.

"Searching for remaining three gunmen. What's your ETA?" he asked his SWAT team lead, Dillon Gray.

He reached the end of the aisle and looked left, then right, before crouching by the endcap. He paused, listening for sounds that might indicate where the gunmen were hiding.

"Roger that," he whispered in answer to the

instructions over the phone. "I've got five customers and four employees locked in the cooler
from the inside with good cover. There are coats
in there, so they're okay for now. Searching for
additional customers. You guys need to get in
here ASAP, full SWAT gear. These yahoos may
be stupid and disorganized. But that makes them
unpredictable and dangerous."

A noise sounded from the east end of the store.
He looked down the next aisle. Clear. He jogged
to another endcap, heading east.

"Negative," he whispered in response to Dillon's next question. "No clue what they want.
As soon as the cashier screamed, they started
shooting. Erratic though, as if they don't know
how to handle those M16s they're waving around.
Thankfully no one's been hit yet except the one
gunman I took out."

With his fellow SWAT team members apprised
of the situation, he put his cell phone away so he
could focus on finding the one customer he knew
was unaccounted for.

Bex.

As PLANS WENT, hiding behind a waist-high
clothing rack of "I Dig the Pig" Piggly Wiggly
T-shirts probably wasn't the best one Bex could
have made. But when she'd seen the end of a rifle
emerging from one of the side aisles, she'd dived

behind the closest cover she could find. Unfortunately, the T-shirts were apparently good sellers. There were barely enough left to conceal her.

She held her breath as the gunman crept past her hiding space. He was dressed in black jeans and a black T-shirt and was wearing sunglasses. She supposed that was his idea of a disguise, but he clearly was young—probably barely out of high school. The other gunman she'd seen a few minutes ago had a black ski mask over his face and the build of someone older, maybe late twenties. Both of them were carrying wicked-looking rifles.

The guy in sunglasses turned down the aisle she'd left just a minute earlier. She let out a shaky breath, then crept to the side of the display, ready to zip down another aisle to get to the front of the store. That's where she'd last heard the sound of a pistol. And she was betting that pistol belonged to Max.

She leaned forward, looked left, right, then—*oomph!* A hand clamped over her mouth and she was yanked backward behind the shirts.

Chapter Three

Bex struggled against her captor, twisting and writhing in his grasp.

He pressed his cheek against hers and held her so tight she could barely move.

"Be still, Bex. It's me, Max."

She froze, then went limp with relief.

He slowly lifted his hand from her mouth, as if he didn't quite trust her not to cry out. She half turned to look at him, nodding to let him know she wasn't going to sob hysterically and give away their position. Or at least she didn't think she was. Cowering from gunmen was an entirely new experience for her. She could very well start screaming like a madwoman any second.

Apparently Max had more faith in her than she did. He loosened his arm around her waist and let her go. She was about to ask him what she should do when he edged to the right of the display. His whole body was tense, alert, as ducked lower and slid his pistol into the holster at his waist. What was he doing?

A gunman, the one in the ski mask, stepped out from behind a stack of bagels and English muffins, his gaze zeroing in on Bex through a gap in the clothing rack. She ducked behind another shirt, expecting to feel a bullet slam into her any second. The gunman rushed forward, his sneakers visible beneath the clothes.

Bex jerked her head toward Max. But he wasn't even looking at her. He was poised like a runner, one leg down, one up, balancing on his fingertips like he was about to take off in a sprint. Ski mask guy stopped directly in front of the rack, looking down at Bex. He started to raise his gun.

She squeezed her eyes shut. The air rushed beside her. The squeak of a shoe sounded on the floor. She heard a grunt, then…nothing. She was still alive. No bullets had ripped into her body and thrown her to the floor in a pool of her own blood.

"Bex," a harsh whisper sounded. "Move. Now."

Her eyes flew open. Impossibly, Max stood towering over her, ski mask guy hanging limply over his shoulder, his arms dangling toward the ground. Max jerked his head, motioning for her to run to the aisle directly across from them.

Stunned that she was still alive and *could* run,

she darted forward, stopping a few feet down the aisle and looking back.

Max was lowering the unconscious—dead?—gunman to the floor under the rack. Bex swallowed, hard. Moments later, Max stopped beside her with a confiscated rifle in his hand.

He frowned. "Are you all right?"

She looked past him at the body visible beneath the obscenely cheery pink and green shirts. A shiver ran up her spine over their close call but she forced a nod.

After a quick look to the far end of their row, Max checked the rifle's loading, then yanked out his pistol and shoved it toward her.

"Remember how to use one of these?" he whispered.

She swallowed. "Sure. But I haven't fired one in years."

Something dark passed in his eyes, and she knew he was remembering one of the many times long ago when he'd taken her to target practice. When other boys waffled between wanting to be a pilot or a fireman or maybe a professional football player, Max had never wavered in his desire to be a detective and SWAT officer like cool Chief Thornton, who'd visited Destiny High every year on career day.

Max had loved the idea of piecing clues together and solving crimes as his main gig. And then, when the situation called for it, putting on full SWAT gear and storming some criminal's compound to rescue hostages. It had been his dream. And seeing him now, so calm and focused, she knew that if anyone could save her and the other customers, it was Max. But only if she followed his instructions and let him do his job.

She took the pistol, careful to point it away from him and keep her finger on the frame, not the trigger, as he'd drilled into her so many times.

He gave her a nod of approval and pivoted toward the back of the store again, then the front, as if scoping out their situation. Then he dropped to his knees and peered in between the bottom shelf and the one above it on both sides of the aisle they were on. He hesitated, as if thinking something through. Then he was pushing boxes of noodles and pasta behind the jars of spaghetti sauce. When he'd cleared a spot a couple of feet wide, he grabbed her arms and shoved her toward the opening.

She wanted to protest that she wasn't nearly as small as he apparently thought she was. But the sound of footsteps, and Max's head jerking toward the front of the store, had her squeezing into the impossibly small hole and pulling her legs in after her as tightly as she could. The sharp scrape of the metal shelf against her arm had her clenching her teeth. But she didn't make a sound.

He leaned down, held a finger to his lips motioning for her to be quiet, and then he was gone.

She clutched the pistol in both hands, her pulse pounding so hard she felt light-headed. A tiny tapping sound started above her head. She twisted to see what was causing it and realized she was shaking so hard her shoulders were making the shelving above her rattle against its brackets. She drew several deep, slow breaths and concentrated on trying to calm down. The tapping stopped. Then she heard it, another sound—footsteps.

Coming toward her.

Her finger shook as she moved it to the trigger. Wait. It could be Max. She moved her finger back to the gun's frame.

Oh, God. Please let it be Max coming back for her.

The tapping started again. She clamped her jaw and forced herself to hold still. The footsteps stopped. Was it one of the gunmen? Had he heard her?

Ever so carefully, she peeked through the gap above the boxes of pasta to her left but couldn't see more than a few feet. Looking the other way yielded more of the same—boxes and jars blocking her view.

A squeak. Someone's shoe against the floor?

Her hand started shaking violently, the pistol bobbing in her grip. A trickle of sweat rolled down the side of her face.

Another sound. *Oh, God.* Someone was behind her. She was surrounded. The person in her aisle shuffled forward, his shoes squeaking again.

Bam! Bam! Bam!

Gunfire sounded from the front of the store. She sucked in a breath.

Bang!

Another shot rang out.

A new sound—scuffling feet not far from her hiding place. A muffled curse. A dull crack. More footsteps, hurrying toward her now.

This was it. He was coming for her.

She steadied the pistol, blew her breath out, tried to remember everything Max had taught her all those years ago. Exhale slowly, move your finger to the trigger, squeeze—

"Bex, it's me. Don't shoot."

She blinked. Max? Wait, he wasn't whispering.

She moved her finger away from the trigger just as he crouched down in front of her and peered into her hiding place.

"Max?" All of her questions and fears were in that one hoarsely uttered word.

"It's okay," he said. "It's over."

He gently took the pistol from her violently shaking hands, shoved it into his holster. And then he was scooping his arms beneath her, pulling her out of the maze of pasta and sauces and lifting her up against his chest.

The sight of a dark heap on the floor had her throwing her arms around Max's neck and squeezing her eyes tightly shut.

"Is he...is he—"

"He's alive. Don't worry about him. I've got you, Bex. Everything's going to be all right."

She should have told him to put her down, that she was perfectly capable of walking on her own. But she wasn't entirely sure that was true. Her whole body seemed to have turned into a mass of shaking nerves. She squeezed her eyes tightly shut and selfishly buried her face against Max's chest while he carried her to the front of the store.

She sensed others around them now, heard someone ask Max something but didn't catch his murmured reply. More sounds—voices, boots scuffling across the floor. Her traumatized mind grasped what was happening, that help had finally arrived, that the SWAT team must be clearing the store and securing the scene. But she couldn't seem to force her eyes open or loosen her grip around Max's neck as he carried her outside.

Chapter Four

Max leaned against a Destiny PD patrol car in the Piggly Wiggly parking lot, in a circle with the five other officers who made up the SWAT team, all in full tactical gear except him. Since the danger was over, they were talking in detective mode, trying to figure out what had just happened.

There'd been no fatalities. The only people to get shot were two of the gunmen, courtesy of Max, and they were on their way to the hospital. The three other bad guys were on their way to the county lockup. But the grocery store and surrounding area were still bustling with firefighters and police officers and would be for quite a while as they sorted through the mess.

Chief Thornton, who'd been talking to the fire chief, shoved his way between team lead Dillon Gray and his best friend, second in command Chris Downing. The others—Donna Waters,

Colby Vale and Randy Carter—widened the circle to make room.

Thornton looked at each of them, a ferocious frown on his brow. "Where's the new guy?"

Max's lips twitched at the shrugs and carefully blank looks on Dillon's and Chris's faces. The chief was having a heck of a time trying to force everyone to accept a new member onto their SWAT team and detective squad. Blake Sullivan was still learning the ropes of Destiny PD and no one was exactly rolling out a welcome mat for him.

The guy was former military and had been a detective in Knoxville before relocating here. He'd made it clear on his first day that he expected to step right into the action. It had been a bitter pill for him to realize he had to spend several months as a uniformed beat cop first—as they all had—to learn the station's routine and his way around the county before becoming an active member of the team.

Thornton turned around, looking for his beleaguered new hire, then put his hands on his hips. He'd obviously spotted Blake, fifty yards away, looking bored as he leaned against the ambulance where Bex was being examined by an EMT.

"Why isn't he wearing tactical gear like the rest of you?" Thornton demanded, directing his question at Dillon.

"When Max's call came in, we had to hustle,"

Dillon said. "Didn't have time to coddle a new-bie and bring him in on the assault."

The chief narrowed his eyes. "This would have been a perfect opportunity to show him the ropes. Next time the team is activated, you had better include him. You hear me?"

"Yes, sir. I hear you."

Max grinned. He wouldn't bet a plug nickel that Blake would be included on their next call-out. At this point, it was a matter of principle. Blake would have to show some humility before Dillon would back down. And judging by how distant and arrogant the new guy seemed most of the time, that moment of acceptance wasn't going to happen anytime soon.

"Colby, go get Blake." The chief jerked his head toward the ambulance.

Colby sighed and jogged across the parking lot.

"And you, Max, stop grinning like the village idiot and tell me if you recognize any of the gun-men. Chris snapped their pictures as they were brought out, minus the ski masks and sunglasses some of them were wearing." The chief motioned for Chris to pass his phone to Max.

Max flipped through the images on the screen, then shook his head and returned the phone to Chris.

"None of them look familiar. I don't think they're local."

"He's right," Dillon said, not even glancing Blake's way as Colby ushered him into their circle. "We all grew up here. I may not know everyone in town by name, but I know most of them by sight. I've never seen any of those men before."

"Let me have a look." Blake held out his hand.

Chris arched a brow.

Max shoved him. "Give him a break. What could it hurt?"

Chris shoved him back but handed his phone over.

Blake's jaw tightened. One of these days the guy would probably explode like a spring that had been wound too tight. Max wasn't sure he wanted to be there when that happened.

"Well?" the chief asked, impatience heavy in his tone as Blake carefully examined each picture.

He handed the phone to Chris. "The second one and the last one are gangbangers from my hometown. I don't know their names. But they have the same tattoos on their forearms as other gangbangers I've arrested."

"They're gang members from Knoxville?" the chief asked.

Blake nodded. "Those two for sure. Can't speak for the other three. I can call my old squad, send them the photos to help us get IDs. Maybe the other ones just don't have their tats yet. They have to earn them. But we can assume they're all in the same gang."

"We don't assume anything around here," Dillon said. "We deal in facts."

Blake's shoulders stiffened, but he didn't rise to the bait.

Colby asked, "Why would street thugs drive forty-five minutes to storm a small, rural grocery store with assault rifles? They could have made a much bigger haul in Knoxville."

"They didn't get a haul at all. Didn't even try," Max said. "As soon as they came in, they started firing wildly into the air—except the one who shot at me. They split up as if looking for something, leaving only two guys to control the customers up front. But they didn't seem to have a clue what they were doing. I was able to signal the manager to hustle the employees and customers into the cooler while I drew the gunmen's fire. If they were there for money, they'd have all stayed up front and forced the manager to open the safe."

Dillon crossed his arms, looking thoughtful. "They came here looking for something."

"Maybe they were looking for some*one*." Max nodded toward the other end of the parking lot.

As one they all turned to see Bex, still sitting in the back of an ambulance.

The chief motioned to Chris. "Text those pictures to all of our phones. Max, show the pics to

Miss Kane and ask her whether she recognizes any of them."

Max straightened away from the cruiser. "Dillon's the lead. He should question her."

A look of surprise flashed across Dillon's face, but he took a step toward Bex anyway.

The chief put his hand on Dillon's shoulder to stop him. "No. Max is going to interview her. The rest of you can change out of your gear and get initial statements from the other witnesses. The EMTs should be done checking them out soon. One of our officers is putting them in the break room as their medical reviews are done, unless any of them need to be hospitalized. You know the routine. Get those statements."

Colby clapped Max on the shoulder in a show of solidarity as he and the others headed to their vehicles to shed their gear. When only the chief remained, he faced Max with his hands on his hips.

"Go on, son. Spit it out. You look like you're chewing on nails."

"You, more than anyone, know my history. You hired me right out of high school, right after... everything. Dillon or one of the others should interview Miss Kane. Not me."

"That it? That's all you got to say?"

He wanted to say a whole lot more. But he

respected his boss too much to let loose with a string of curses. "Yes, sir. That about sums it up."

"Good. Glad we got that settled. Because you're a professional and I've never had reason to say otherwise. Don't give me a reason today. Miss Kane was clinging to you like a lifeline when you carried her out of the store and it took ten minutes of your sweet-talking to get her to let you go. You may not be comfortable, given your past. And I understand that, I really do. But this isn't about you. This is about finding the truth, conducting an investigation. Right now, whether either of us likes it or not, you're our best option for getting her to answer our questions. Now, I ain't normally one to explain my decisions and don't plan on doing this again anytime soon. So I suggest you get over there and *do your job, Detective.*"

Heat flushed up his neck. His face was probably beet red. Feeling like a high school kid who'd just been scolded by the principal for skipping class, Max gave his boss a curt nod and strode across the parking lot.

Before Max was even halfway there, he noticed an older gentleman in a dark gray suit working his way between the cars and fire trucks toward Bex's ambulance. Max hesitated. The man was Augustus Leonard, one of only two lawyers in town. Why did a lawyer want to talk to Bex?

THE EMT, DON, steadied Bex's left forearm on a raised metal board that he'd slid out from the wall of the ambulance. From the amount of bandages, antibiotic sprays and other first aid equipment lying around, Bex would have thought her arm had been severed. She was embarrassed at all the fuss he was making over such a small cut.

Pausing with a needle poised between what looked like tweezers, he said, "Ma'am, are you sure you won't go to the hospital and have a doctor stitch you up? You may need X-rays. There might be other injuries you don't even know about yet."

She shook her head. "I don't have anything more serious than this."

"You're one lucky woman. It could've been a lot worse."

Bits of memories flashed through her mind—gunshots, crouching behind the T-shirt rack, her stomach clenching with dread as the gunman with the ski mask raised his arm, ready to shoot her. She shivered and considered the bandage on her arm. He was right. It could have been so much worse.

"You're right. And I assure you I'm very grateful that I'm only getting stitches."

"Stitches? What stitches?" a gravelly voice said from the open doors of the ambulance.

Bex looked over, smiling to see her lawyer

looking all proper and perfect, his white hair neatly in place, his handlebar mustache sticking out on each side like skinny white toothpicks. She started to lean toward him to shake his hand, but Don frowned at her, holding her injured arm steady.

"Sorry, Don." She waved at her lawyer. "Mr. Leonard, nice to see you. What are you doing here?"

He arched a bushy brow. "I might ask you the same thing, Miss Kane. Imagine my concern when I look out my office window and see a SWAT team racing into the grocery store. Even worse, a few minutes later, you're carried out by Detective Remington and placed in this ambulance. And now I hear something about stitches. Do tell, please, what's going on? How badly are you hurt?"

She nodded toward her left arm. "Not bad at all. Just about to get a couple of stitches, that's all."

"More than a couple," the EMT murmured as he pricked her skin with the needle.

The shot he'd given her to numb her arm did its job, but she couldn't help wincing and looking away.

"How did you get cut?" her lawyer asked.

"It happened when I crawled in between some shelves. Some gunmen held up the store and I had to hide. I really am okay. Thanks to Max—ah, Detective Remington."

"Who else was hurt?" he asked. "I saw two men brought out on stretchers."

"I have no idea. I haven't heard about anyone else in the store, or the details about what happened. I hope those men will be okay."

"They were the bad guys," Don said without glancing up from his work. "Heard it over the radio. Two of the gunmen were shot and taken to Maryville. I don't think any of the shoppers were injured."

Bex turned her head again as he poked the needle into her skin.

"Hurts?" Augustus asked.

"No, I just…don't like needles."

"It's a shame your mother refused to let you come see her in Destiny all these years and then your first time back you end up in the middle of a robbery." He shook his head. "Dorothy shouldn't have kept you from your own home all this time. It wasn't right. For what it's worth, I did try to talk some sense into her. But she was too worried about you, was determined to keep you away."

"I just wish she would have agreed to move in with me. But she insisted on staying here," Bex said.

"Destiny was her home. She had a lot of friends

here, her volunteer work at the church. I doubt she'd have moved for anyone."

"Well, I guess it all worked out. Mama enjoyed the trips to see me. She got a little thrill every time I had a limo pick her up."

"You spoiled her."

"She deserved it. I only wish I could have done more for her while she was alive. No matter how well my business did, she refused to let me buy her anything expensive. Half the gifts I mailed her were returned. I sent her a houseful of furniture once and she wouldn't sign for it, wouldn't even let the guys unload anything from the truck."

He smiled. "That's Dorothy for you." He leaned forward and patted her good hand. "My condolences again. I know you loved her very much. Her heart attack was such a shock to us all."

She blinked against the burn of unshed tears. "Thank you. No sense in dwelling on the past anymore, though. I need to wrap things up here and get back to my own home as soon as I can, make sure Allison isn't ready to quit after being left in charge of the antique shop so long."

"Allison?"

"My assistant. And friend. Once I pack up everything, when do you think I'll be able to put the house up for sale?"

She risked a quick look at her injured arm. Four

stitches in, probably a few more to go. She looked away before Don dipped the needle in again.

"Another few weeks at best, a month at the worst. Your mother's will is fairly straightforward. But there are some tangles to unravel with the various properties she had around the county and ensuring there are no liens before I can get them transferred to you as the owner."

"You're referring to the farmland my daddy used to have? Aren't those plots leased out to local farmers? The same ones who've been on that land since Daddy died years ago?"

"Yes, but it won't take long to clear them out. Shouldn't be a problem. It's a standard eviction process."

"I don't want them cleared out. Just transfer the deeds to them."

He blinked like an owl. "Pardon?"

"I don't need the land, Mr. Leonard. And I'm doing well with my antique store. I'm not rich by any stretch. But I've got what I need. No reason to be greedy. Those men have worked that land for years. They've earned this. It's the right thing to do. Mom and Dad would approve, I'm sure."

He looked like he wanted to argue but he gave her a crisp nod. "Very well. It's your land, your money. I'll draw up some papers to make the transfer. It will take more time than originally planned, of course."

"Thank you. I understand."

Don jostled her arm as he leaned past her to put away the needle. But when she started to pull back, he stopped her.

"I need to bandage that before we're done," he said.

She sighed and relaxed her arm.

Don cleaned up the tabletop to prepare for bandaging her cut.

"If the paperwork takes much longer, can we plan on doing it through the mail? Including the sale of my mom's house?"

He frowned. "Why would you want to do that? You're here now. If a few more weeks is too long, I can try to put a rush on things."

"I don't want you to have to hurry on my account. But after, well, after today, I'm more inclined to finish packing up the house and just go. Can't I sign some kind of power of attorney over to you?"

His brows raised again, making her think of snow-white caterpillars.

"You can, certainly. But most people prefer to give power of attorney to someone they know and trust rather than to their lawyer."

"My mama trusted you. That's good enough for me."

He puffed out his chest, his face turning a light shade of red. And suddenly Bex wondered whether he'd felt more toward her mother than simple friendship. And whether those feelings were returned. If so, her mother had never said anything. But then again, her mother might have worried that Bex would feel funny about her finally dating someone after all these years. And, truth be told, she would have felt…odd about it.

A car crash had taken Bex's father from them when Bex was in middle school. The loss had been devastating for her and her mother. Imagining her mom with anyone other than her daddy made her feel sad. But happy, too. Her mother deserved some male companionship in her life. And if she'd found it with the honorable Mr. Augustus Leonard, then that was a very good thing.

Mr. Leonard cleared his throat. "Thank you for your faith in me, Miss Kane. I have a form at the office you can fill out for the power of attorney. When you're finished here, I can walk you over. Martha's a notary. She can witness our signatures and notarize the document."

"Can you raise your arm a few inches?" Don asked.

Bex lifted her arm so he could wrap some gauze over the stitches.

"Sounds like a plan," she said to her lawyer.

"The sooner I can get out of Destiny the better. There's nothing left for me here except bad memories."

Movement near the ambulance doors had her looking up, and right into Max's eyes. Again. And just like in the grocery store, his jaw tightened and his eyes darkened.

"Max. Um, hi. How long have you been standing there?" she asked.

"Long enough." The bitterness in his voice surprised her. Had he heard what she'd said to Mr. Leonard? Why would it matter? He certainly didn't have any feelings for her anymore, as evidenced by how he'd treated her at the deli.

Or did he?

He motioned toward the bandage. "What's wrong with your arm?"

She blinked and looked down, having forgotten all about her injured arm. "It's just a little cut."

"More like a gash," Don said. "Eight stitches."

"How did that happen?" Max elbowed his way past the lawyer and hopped into the ambulance. He grabbed Bex's left hand to inspect the EMT's work as if he would demand a redo if it didn't meet his standards.

Bex frowned and tugged her arm out of his grasp. "I assume it happened when you…when I hid between the shelves. It's not a big deal. I'm fine. Really."

He studied her a moment, then promptly ignored her, speaking instead to the EMT.

"Why didn't you take her to the hospital?"

"She said she didn't—"

"I refused to go to the hospital," she said.

"Well?" he asked the EMT, as if she hadn't spoken.

Don's brows rose to his hairline. "I, ah, Miss Kane didn't want to go to the hospital. She asked me if I could take care of her arm here."

"What about the risk of infection? Those grocery store shelves aren't exactly sterile."

The bewildered look on Don's face hardened. "I know how to clean a wound, sir. And I asked Miss Kane about getting a tetanus shot, but she insisted that she didn't need one."

Max turned to face her. "You either get the shot or you're going to the hospital."

Bex rolled her eyes and grabbed her purse from the bench beside her.

"I'm not an idiot, Max. I'm up-to-date on my shots. And I don't need you, or anyone else, bossing me around." She shook the EMT's hand. "Thank you, Don. I appreciate your help."

She went to hop down from the ambulance, but Max gently pushed her back and hopped down first. Then he lifted her out before she realized what he was about to do.

The feel of his warm hands around her sent a

delightful shock of awareness up her spine, making her stiffen in surprise.

His jaw tightened and he dropped his hands, taking a quick step back. Before she could correct his obvious misinterpretation of her reaction, Mr. Leonard stepped forward.

"I'll escort you back to my office."

"She needs to answer some questions about the shooting," Max said, a thread of steel in his deep voice.

Eager to avoid any kind of confrontation, Bex stepped between the two men and shook Mr. Leonard's hand. "Thank you, for everything. If you don't mind, I'll go to your office some other time to sign that power of attorney."

"Very well. My door's always open for you, Miss Kane." He tipped his head politely. "Detective Remington." Then he headed across the parking lot toward his office, one of a handful of businesses and restaurants on Magnolia Street.

Max waved Bex back from the ambulance so Don could close the doors and prepare to return to the hospital.

Bex crossed her arms, not quite sure which Max Remington was standing before her now— the one full of anger at the deli, or the one who'd nearly broken her heart with kindness as he'd soothed her after carrying her out of the store.

"I never really thanked you before. You saved my life today."

"Just doing my job." His voice was curt, clipped.

She sighed. Deli Max was back.

"Chief Thornton wants me to show you some pictures of the gunmen to see whether you recognize them. And I'm sure he'll want me to interview you about what happened," he continued. "I figure it will be easier at the station. We can take my truck. I'll bring you back to your car when we're done."

He reached for her good arm, but she jerked back, her stomach churning with dread. At the mention of the police station, her body flushed with heat, in spite of the chill in the air. She shook her head and took a step away from him.

"I'm not going to the police station."

He frowned. "Why not?"

She glanced past him at Thornton, who was talking to a uniformed officer about thirty yards away. "I…don't have fond memories of that place, as you can imagine. And I never intend to go there again. So, unless you're arresting me, the answer is no."

She hurried toward her car, which, thankfully, was no longer blocked by a fire engine, as it had been earlier.

"Bex. Wait."

The irritation in his voice as he followed her

had her practically running and pulling out her keys. She stopped beside a blue Honda and reached for the door handle just as Max caught up to her. He braced a hip against the door and crossed his arms as if daring her to try to open it.

Which was fine, since this wasn't her car.

She stepped back, her hands on her hips. Then she took another step, then whirled around and ran to her Toyota RAV4 SUV two spaces over. By the time Max realized she'd played a trick on him and started toward her, she was zipping out of the parking space.

He stood watching her in her rearview mirror, his hands fisted at his sides.

Running from him was childish. Especially since he was a police officer and she'd have to answer his questions eventually. But facing angry, cold Max was more than she could take right now after everything else that had happened. How could she stand there, talking to him as if he was a stranger, when even now her body yearned for his touch?

It might have been ten years since she'd last kissed him, a decade since she'd felt the comforting weight of his body pressing her down into the mattress. But from the moment she'd seen him at the deli, all those years had fallen away as if they'd never happened. And her emotions were just as raw now as the day she'd left.

She wanted, needed, some time to herself. To decompress, to reflect about what had happened today and get her emotions back under control. Trying to do that with a man she'd once loved looking at her like he despised her was more than she could bear, more than anyone should have to bear after the kind of crisis she'd just lived through. No, tomorrow would be soon enough. She'd face Max tomorrow.

The sound of a powerful engine had her looking in her rearview mirror again. A shiny black four-by-four pickup was coming up fast behind her. And sitting in the driver's seat was an achingly familiar silhouette.

Max Remington.

Chapter Five

Normally the ride from the grocery store to her mother's house would have taken Bex twenty-five minutes. Today, with Max riding her bumper, it took half that. She barreled into the driveway on the left side of the house and slammed her brakes. Max braked hard behind her, narrowly missing her car.

He hopped out of his pickup and stalked up to her window before she'd even cut her engine.

"Get out."

Even with the window rolled up, she could hear the anger vibrating in his deep voice.

"Go away."

He shook his head. "Open the door, Bex."

She gave him a very unladylike gesture and reached for the gearshift, fully intending to drive across the lawn back to the road.

"Gonna run again, Bex?" he taunted. "You're good at that."

She stiffened.

"You drove twenty miles over the speed limit. I can arrest you for that."

"There was a maniac following me. I was in fear for my life."

If his jaw tightened any more his teeth would probably break.

A long breath huffed out of her as her anger drained away. This wasn't how she wanted things between the two of them. She'd blindsided him by coming back and deserved a little consideration. He'd also saved her life today. Repaying him by pushing his buttons and making his job difficult wasn't right. She cut the engine, grabbed her purse and waited.

Looking suspicious at her sudden change of heart, he seemed to almost reluctantly step back, just enough for her to open the door and get out of her car.

As she headed toward the wide, covered front porch than ran the width of the cottage, he was hot on her heels, so close she could feel his body heat against her back. And just like that, her skin prickled with awareness and her belly tightened, her body's natural response to Max being that close.

She couldn't believe he still had this kind of impact on her, after all these years and after everything that had happened. It was irritating, and made it really hard to keep her raw emotions at bay.

"You don't have to hang so close," she told him as she climbed the steps.

"Just making sure you don't run again," he taunted.

She stopped, then whirled around to face him. But he was too close. She had to climb two more steps to be able to meet his gaze without craning her head back.

"Was that supposed to be funny?" she demanded.

"Not even a little bit."

He arched a brow, daring her to bring up the past, to go down a road she had no intention of traveling. Down that road lay too much hurt. And danger. For both of them.

She let out a pent-up breath and turned around, climbing the rest of the steps and crossing the wide porch. After unlocking the front door, she turned the knob. And suddenly he was pushing past her into the living room.

"Please, won't you come in," she muttered behind him, closing the door and flipping the dead bolt.

He did a quick turn around the room, glancing through doorways into the kitchen, the hall, the bathroom, all while keeping his hand on his holster. She supposed it was second nature to do things like that, the instincts of a cop automatically checking the security when they went anywhere.

When he returned to the entry, he eyed the dead bolt but didn't say the obvious—that she'd never have locked a door when she was growing up here. Most people in Destiny didn't lock their doors. Bex's mother certainly hadn't. The dead bolt had been frozen when Bex had arrived and she'd had to spray it with oil to get it to work.

Feeling silly now for having locked it, she flipped the bolt again, leaving the door unsecured, even though her big city instincts had her fingers itching to flip the bolt.

For a man who'd been all bent out of shape about wanting to talk to her, Max didn't seem to be in any kind of hurry to talk now. Instead, he strolled around the room, examining the stacks of boxes containing her mother's things, reading the labels on each one. When he reached the fireplace, he stared in silence at the dark square above it where a picture of the two of them from their senior prom used to hang. She expected him to ask her what she'd done with it, perhaps in a sarcastic or accusing tone. She'd die before she told him that she'd carefully packed it away and put it in a box to go back home with her to Knoxville. But he didn't ask.

Instead, he turned around and headed toward

the archway that led into the eat-in kitchen on the front left side of the house.

"Got any coffee? I sure could use some even though it's inching toward dinnertime now," he said.

She frowned and hurried after him. "I thought you wanted to interview me about what happened at the store? Show me some pictures or something?"

He hesitated, then pulled his phone out. A moment later, he flipped through pictures of five men, holding each one up for her.

"Recognize any of them?"

"No. Are those the gunmen?"

He didn't answer, just put his phone back in his pocket. After opening the cabinet to the right of the sink, he took down two coffee cups, acting just as familiar and comfortable with the house as he'd been as a teenager. As if the years between had never happened.

A few minutes later he had the old-fashioned coffeemaker spitting and gurgling a thin stream of dark coffee into a carafe.

"Cream and sugar still?" He took the creamer out of the refrigerator, which Bex had topped off just this morning, and grabbed the sugar bowl from the kitchen table.

"Yes. Still." She pulled out one of the chairs

and plopped down. "I'm surprised you remember where Mom kept everything."

His lips thinned. "I practically lived here in high school. Your mom was like a second mom to me. We kept in touch. I didn't write her out of my life just because you wrote me out of yours."

She sucked in a breath, old hurts washing over her. The last time she'd seen Max suddenly felt just as fresh and painful as it had the first time around—as if all the years in between had never happened. She should apologize, explain. He deserved that. But how could she?

Especially now that he was a cop.

He set the cup of creamy white coffee in front of her and a cup of strong, black coffee in front of himself before finally sitting across from her.

He rubbed his neck and let out a deep sigh, stretching his long legs out in front of him. He looked so tired, as if the weight of everything that had happened today had drained the fight right out of him.

"Why did you come back, Bex? After all these years, why come back at all? It's not like you went to the memorial service."

She almost choked on the coffee she'd just sipped. She forced the now tasteless liquid down her throat and shoved the cup away. She rose from her chair, fully intending to order him to leave.

"Bex. Please. I'm not trying to fight. I really want to know." He watched her intently, waiting for her to make the decision.

She drew a deep breath then sat down again. "I had a private funeral for her in...outside Destiny."

He nodded. "I figured. Which is kind of my point. Why come back? You didn't have to. You could handle everything remotely. From wherever you live now."

Silence filled the room, his unasked questions hanging between them. Where did she live? Where had she gone? Where would she go once she left again?

She considered telling him. It wasn't exactly a big secret anymore, as it had been when she'd fled. Privacy was a fantasy these days. Finding someone was as easy as doing a search online, even if they'd changed their name—which she hadn't done.

If Max really wanted to find her, he could. Especially as a police officer. He'd be able to track her down. And yet, all these years, he'd never once tried to find her. Had never walked up to her condo or visited her little shop, asking for answers. So she wasn't going to give them now.

"I needed to settle her estate, go through her things, pack up the house."

He didn't say anything, just waited.

She glanced around the kitchen, at the fading yellow drapes hanging above the sink. The horrible red-rooster wallpaper on the wall above the stove, wallpaper that she'd hated while growing up here but that somehow seemed perfect now.

She smoothed her fingers against the faded, chipped laminate-topped table. Her mother had refused to let Bex replace it with one of the gorgeous antiques from her store. Mom had insisted she loved the cheap, worn table. But Bex knew that what her mom really loved were the memories she'd shared with Bex's father at this worn-out table, before a tight curve on a dark road had taken him away from both of them.

"Bex?"

She forced her hands to stop rubbing circles on the fake wood. "I guess I just…needed to see… home, one last time. I wanted to go through her things, remember her, decide what to keep, what to give away."

"Was there any other reason that you came back?" he asked, his deep voice soft, barely above a whisper.

He was giving her an opening. It shocked her to realize that, to see the longing in his eyes, bared before her. And, God help her, she wanted so much to tell him that, yes, she came back to see him, too. But that wasn't true. No matter how much she wished it could be. Once she left this time, she knew she'd never see Max again.

She slowly shook her head. "No. No other reason."

He blinked, and like throwing a switch, his eyes shuttered, his expression went blank. "Well," he finally said. "Guess that answers that." He gave her a bitter smile. "I loved you, Bex. All those years ago, I loved you in every way a man can love a woman—with my mind, my body, my heart, my soul. And I thought you loved me, too. I would have done anything for you back then. Anything. Together we could have faced whatever really happened the night Bobby Caldwell died. We would have gotten married, raised a couple of kids by now." He shook his head, a muscle flexing in his cheek. "But all that's water under the bridge now, isn't it? You've sure as hell moved on. Guess it's high time I moved on, too." He pulled his phone out of his pocket. "If going to the station's too difficult, so be it. We'll do the interview here. You don't mind if I record it, do you?"

She sat as still as a statue, staring at him in shock, reeling from everything he'd just said. And one thing in particular—that it was time he moved on. What did that mean? That in all these years he'd never dated anyone? That he'd been, what, waiting for her?

She'd dated, a handful of times. But her first dates were always last dates. Because no one had ever measured up to Max. She'd never once considered that he might have been existing in that same limbo that she had all this time. And now she wished that she could tell him the truth.

That she hadn't moved on. And never would. That a day hadn't gone by that she didn't think of him.

He arched a brow. "Bex? I've turned on the recording app. Do you consent to having your statement recorded?"

She blinked, then nodded.

"You have to say it out loud."

"Oh, um." She cleared her throat. "Yes, I consent to having my statement recorded."

"Excellent." He shoved the phone to the middle of the table between them. "First we have to get the logistics out of the way. State and spell your first and last name for the recording. Then list your address and place of employment."

She frowned. "Is that really required?"

He nodded.

She sighed and told him what he'd asked, admitting that she lived in Knoxville, giving him the address of her condo. And she told him about her antique store. Then she went on to answer his questions about everything she'd done the day of the grocery store shooting.

The interview started out stilted, on her side at least. But answering his questions was almost a healing therapy for her emotional wounds. It helped her go numb, almost dead inside, and get through this.

Going over the same questions over and over was grueling, tiring and reminiscent of when the chief had grilled her years ago. Thornton had trained Max well. She felt just as guilty this time as she had ten years ago, even though this time she had nothing to feel guilty about.

He finally stopped the recording and put his phone away. "I guess that's it. For now."

Relieved, she grabbed both of their long-empty coffee cups and carried them to the sink. After rinsing them, she turned around. Max was still sitting at the table, studying her as if he had a million more questions and was looking to her for the answers. Afraid that he might start the interview all over again, she headed toward the archway into the family room.

"Thanks again for protecting me this morning." She waved toward the front door. "You can see yourself out. I've got packing to do."

She headed into her bedroom, the one she'd had her whole life until she'd left at eighteen. Taking the master bedroom hadn't even tempted her. It would have felt…weird, sleeping in the room her mother had slept in just a few short weeks ago.

Her suitcase was in the closet, so she grabbed it and dropped it on top of the bed, then flipped it open. She'd packed light, with just a week's worth of clothes, and had laundered everything yesterday. It wouldn't take long before she could head out. She opened the top dresser drawer and grabbed a stack of underwear and bras.

"You're not sticking around?"

Startled, she jumped, then pressed a hand against her chest. Max lounged in the doorway to her bedroom, looking impossibly appealing.

"Sorry," he said, even though he didn't look sorry. "Didn't mean to startle you."

She shoved her armload of underwear into the suitcase and headed to the dresser for more clothes. "I'm going home."

"When?"

An armload of shorts and T-shirts went into the suitcase. "Today. Now. Just as soon as I'm packed."

"Don't you want to stick around and find out why those gunmen went after you?"

She hesitated, her arms full of jeans. "What are you talking about? They robbed the store. You make it sound like it all had something to do with me."

"I'm thinking maybe it did. They didn't rob the

store. They were searching up and down aisles looking for you. At least, that's what it seemed like to me."

She slowly lowered the jeans into the suitcase. "Why would they be looking for me?"

He shrugged, not offering anything else. Probably because it was part of his investigation.

"All the more reason to leave, then." She headed for the closet to get her shoes.

Max wandered around the room, picking up a few odds and ends from her childhood—little horse figurines on her dresser, a cross necklace her mom had given her on her sixteenth birthday. And then he looked up, at the wall over her dresser, and froze.

Bex could feel her face growing warm. "Mom left my room exactly the way it was the day I left."

He was in most of the pictures, with her, because they'd always been together, from middle school on. It seemed that every fun or cherished moment in her life had Max in it—her first dance, the field trip to Animal Kingdom at Disney, playing video games at the arcade in the mall one town over from Destiny. And there was their graduation photo, the last one taken of the two of them. They'd walked together, hand in hand in their black graduation robes, each of them boasting the gold stoles of the National Honor Society. Both of them smiling and happy.

"Figures I'd find you both here, in your bedroom. Just like old times, huh?"

Bex and Max both turned to see Bex's old high school nemesis, Marcia Knolls, standing in the doorway. Max's hand had automatically gone to the gun holstered at his hip, but he relaxed when he saw who was standing there.

"What are you doing in here?" he demanded. "You should have knocked."

"I did. You two were apparently too busy to hear me." She smirked at Max. "Does your girlfriend know about all those police interns you've been screwing?"

Bex blinked, then looked at Max.

His eyes narrowed, and he took a step toward Marcia.

Bex hurried to step between them.

"Marcia, hey. It's been a long time. Is there something I can help you with?"

Marcia glared at her, hands coiled into fists at her sides. Surprisingly, Bex wasn't even mad at her for her crude comment about her and Max. Instead, she felt sorry for her. Marcia was one of those people who'd been miserable the whole time Bex had known her and had blamed others for that misery. It was clear that she hadn't changed, that she was still just as miserable and lonely as she'd been back in high school.

"I heard about the shooting," Marcia said. "Figured I'd stop by and see if you were okay." She glanced at Max. "Looks like you're doing just fine, already slipping back into old habits."

Bex doubted Marcia had stopped by hoping she was okay. If anything, she was looking for some juicy gossip.

"There was a shooting at the Piggly Wiggly. But thanks to Max, everyone is fine. He saved my life, and the lives of everyone else in that store." She could feel the weight of his stare, as if he was surprised or wondering if she really felt that way.

"Yeah, well, too bad he couldn't save everyone years ago," Marcia taunted. "Then maybe Bobby would still be around."

"What do you really want, Marcia?" Max asked. "You can cut the crap about caring about Bex. No one in this room believes that."

She gave him a resentful look. "I was just wondering when Bex plans on leaving." She waved toward the suitcase. "I'm assuming soon?"

"And why do you want to know?" Max demanded.

Her face reddening slightly, Marcia said, "Mama sent me over with a casserole and her condolences on your mother's death, Bex." She cleared her throat. "Not that you really cared, did you? You never bothered to visit her."

Max stepped even closer. "Not that it's any of your business, but Bex saw her mother a lot, just not in Destiny. And they spoke on the phone every Sunday evening, without fail. Now, unless you have something nice to say to a woman who's grieving the loss of her mother, you need to leave."

Bex almost felt sorry for Marcia. Her face went pale and she seemed taken aback. "I wasn't trying to be mean." She aimed a pleading look at Bex. "I'm sorry about your mom. I really am. It's just that when I see you, it makes me think of Bobby. And I just—"

"Out. Now." Max used his much larger body to force her into the hallway.

Bex was about to tell him to go easy on Marcia when the other woman turned and ran from the house. Max followed her, and soon the sound of the front door slamming echoed through the little house.

If she hadn't been anxious to leave before, Bex was anxious now. She'd meant it when she'd told her lawyer that there wasn't any reason left for her to stay. Marcia was only one of many who blamed Bex for Bobby's death. And Max wasn't exactly warming up to her. Not that she could blame him.

Bex stuffed a few more things into her suitcase and zipped it closed.

"She's gone," Max said from the doorway. "You're really leaving, right this minute?"

"I think it's for the best. I'll stop at my lawyer's office in town, then I'm off to Pigeon Forge for a couple of weeks to clear my head before going home."

He was reaching for her suitcase but stopped with his hand on the handle. "Pigeon Forge?"

It dawned on her what he was thinking about, and she belatedly wished she'd thought more carefully before answering him. She nodded and refolded an afghan at the foot of the bed that didn't need folding. Pigeon Forge, nestled in the foothills of the Smoky Mountains, had been their place, where she and Max had gone on many trips their junior and senior year. Always with friends, to satisfy her mom that they were well chaperoned. But she and Max had found plenty of time to sneak away to be together. It had been the happiest time of her life. And it had become her habit since leaving Destiny to go to Pigeon Forge every time her life seemed like it was falling apart. The moment she'd found out about her mother, she'd reserved her usual cabin in the Smokies for once she was finished with her duties in Destiny. Now she wasn't sure it was a good idea anymore. Rather than healing her soul, it just might crush her.

Without a word, Max picked up her suitcase and carried it out of the room.

Bex sighed and followed him, grabbing her purse and car keys along the way.

Once he'd placed the suitcase in her trunk, he straightened and leaned against her car. "I may need to contact you with more questions as the investigation goes on."

"Mr. Leonard has my contact information. He'll be able to get in touch with me."

"It's probably better that you're leaving. Bobby Caldwell's death is a fresh wound again now that you're back in town. A lot of people, like it or not, believe you got away with murder. Marcia's just one of them."

She paused beside the driver's door. "Just like you."

"No."

She looked up at him. "You don't think I killed Bobby?"

He swore and ran a hand through his hair. "Whatever...resentments I have toward you, I never once believed you had anything to do with Bobby's death."

She wasn't sure what to say to that. "You told Marcia I saw my mom, that I called her every week. How did you know that?"

He shrugged. "Small town. Word gets around."

"Only if my mom told someone about it. And

she wasn't the type to gossip, not about me. And her close friends wouldn't share that type of information, not with you. The only way you could have known is if Mom told you."

He didn't say anything.

"You're the one who planted the lilies, aren't you?"

Again, he remained silent. But the truth was in his eyes.

"You really did visit my mom regularly, didn't you, Max? Why?"

He straightened away from her car. "Just because you pushed me out of your life didn't mean your mom did. I always planned on marrying you, Bex. From the moment we started hanging out in middle school. I thought of your mom as my future mother-in-law for so long I couldn't just turn that off when you threw my proposal in my face."

She sucked in a breath. "I didn't throw it in your face."

He waved his hand in the air. "Just go see your lawyer and run off to Pigeon Forge. You've probably got some guy waiting there for you. Don't let me keep you."

She glared up at him, her hands on her hips. "And don't let me keep you from those interns you're sleeping with, either."

His jaw tightened and he held the door open for her.

Her anger evaporated in a shaky sigh. Tears burned at the backs of her eyes. "Can't wait for me to leave, can you, Max?"

Something passed in his eyes—regret? His anger seemed to rush out of him, too, and he looked tired and resigned.

"This is never how I wanted things to be between us. But it's probably for the best, Bex."

She nodded. "I'm just glad you're okay. I was so scared when I heard that gunman saying the cop had interfered and they were going to kill him. I figured that was you. I was so scared. I was trying to find you to warn you when I got trapped behind that display of T-shirts."

"You were looking for me to warn me? Are you insane?"

She stiffened. "Apparently so. Take care, Max. I mean it. I want you to be happy and safe. No matter what you think of me, that has never changed. I've always wanted what was best for you. That was the driving concern in every decision that I made."

He frowned at her words. "Bex, what are you—"

She shook her head, realizing she'd said too much. She stepped into the opening to get in the car. A loud boom sounded and the windshield exploded.

Max grabbed her and shoved her to the ground.

Chapter Six

Max crouched down beside a thick oak tree to examine an impression in the dirt. A shoe print, narrow, small and recent—probably the shooter's. He glanced over his shoulder, just able to see Bex's house through the scrub brush. She was inside now, probably hunkered down in a back bedroom with one of Destiny's finest guarding her. But her car, with its shattered windshield, sat where they'd left it when he'd rushed her inside the house and called his SWAT team. The windshield was in a direct line from where he was, which pretty much confirmed that he'd found where the shooter had stood when he'd tried to kill Bex.

A static sound in his earpiece had him turning around. Twenty feet away, at his two o'clock, Colby crouched in full SWAT gear like Max was now wearing, and pointed toward Max's eleven o'clock. He held up one finger, then made a circular motion. The shooter was close. Colby had spotted him. Too close to risk speaking into their earpieces, thus the hand signals. Max nodded to let him know he understood, then he looked to his left and made the same motions to Chris, who was also a good twenty feet away.

The rest of the team was out here, too. When Max had called them from Bex's house, the strategy had been set—half the team would approach from the west, driving the shooter back toward the rest of the team. The plan had worked. And now the shooter was trapped between them.

Max waited, glancing from Colby to Chris, until they both signaled that the whole team was in sync. The static crackled in his ear again, and this time he heard Dillon's voice, so low he wouldn't have heard it if he wasn't listening for it.

"Three, two, one, go."

Max crept forward, as silently as possible, in perfect unison with his team. Sweeping his assault rifle out in front of him, he used the scope every few feet, hoping to see what Colby had seen. Five painfully slow minutes later, the shadowy figure of someone peering out from behind a tree, clutching a rifle, had Max freezing in place.

Ever so carefully, he signaled his teammates. Shooter spotted. He also signaled that this was his takedown. He was the closest. Hell, even if he wasn't, he'd have demanded the right to finish this. Bex might not be his anymore, but he still cared about her—a fact that had been ruthlessly revealed to him today. And he wasn't about to stand by while someone else took down whoever had tried to kill her. No, this shooter was his. And they were definitely going down.

Realizing the rifle was too bulky and cumbersome for such close quarters, he carefully set it against a tree. Then he pulled his pistol from his holster, motioned to his teammates and started forward.

The shooter ducked back behind the tree. Had Max been spotted? He stopped, listened, waited. When he didn't see or hear anything, he started forward again.

Fifteen feet.

Fourteen.

Thirteen.

Something snapped up ahead. He froze. Was that a twig? Or had someone just ratcheted a round into a chamber?

Sweeping his pistol in front of him, he scanned the trees to his left, right. Chris and Colby were still within sight, just barely. They'd stopped, like him, and were waiting, listening.

Two minutes later, Max signaled his teammates and started forward again. His gaze was riveted on the tree where he'd last seen that shadow.

Steady and slow, inch by inch. He stopped a

yard back from the thick tree. Breathing through his mouth, as quietly as possible. He played the waiting game once again. Then he heard it. Fast, shallow breaths. His prey was still exactly where he'd seen him, hiding behind the tree. And from the sound of it, he was practically hyperventilating—afraid.

Good. Max wanted him to experience fear, just like Bex had felt. He was about to spring around the tree when he spotted another shadow, a good thirty feet in front of him. The quick hand signal told him it was Dillon. And then the shadow disappeared behind cover. Dillon was letting Max know that he was close and in the line of fire. Time to switch strategies.

Max ever so carefully holstered his pistol. Then he slowly and quietly pulled the long serrated hunting knife from his boot. He listened to the shallow, rapid breathing. Crept a foot to his left, planning his approach. Without taking his gaze from the tree, he held a hand up in the air, letting his teammates know he was about to strike.

Three.

Two.

One.

He rushed forward, swinging around the tree. Wide, terrified eyes met his. He registered the identity of the shooter a millisecond before he struck, knocking the shooter's rifle skyward and dropping the unneeded knife to the ground as he tackled his prey.

The capture was far too easy for Max's liking. He'd wanted, needed, that explosion of violence against the person who'd nearly killed Bex. But his thirst for vengeance had been discarded the instant he'd seen how scared and pale his opponent was and realized there would be no fighting back.

Underbrush crashed around him from all sides as the rest of the SWAT team swooped out of their hiding places and aimed their rifles toward Max's prisoner.

Marcia Knolls stared up at them, at the guns pointing at her head, then projectile vomited on Max's vest.

MAX STOOD NAKED from the waist up in front of Bex's guest bathroom sink, trying one last time to scrub the stained, reeking fabric of his bullet-resistant vest. Thanks to an always-packed go-bag in his truck, he had a fresh shirt hanging over one of the towel racks. But he didn't want to risk getting it soiled, so he hadn't put it on yet. He scrubbed at the cloth on the vest one more time, then, realizing it was pointless, he swore and tossed it to the floor.

"I could have told you it was a lost cause." Dillon stood in the bathroom doorway, a grin on his face. "Trade it with Blake. You two are about the same size."

"Yeah, I'm sure he wants a vest that smells like vomit."

Dillon shrugged. "As a newbie, you take what you can get."

"You don't really mean that."

Dillon shrugged again. But Max knew he was right, that their team leader wouldn't try to give Max's ruined vest to the rookie. Dillon might be playing hardball right now with Blake, but he didn't play dirty.

Max rested his hands on the countertop as he looked at Dillon in the mirror. "Speaking of Blake—"

"Yeah, yeah. I know. The chief is going to be ticked. But, honestly, this time I completely forgot about the guy. It didn't even occur to me to include him on the callout."

Max laughed.

Dillon frowned. "It's not funny. I'm going to get a thirty-minute lecture out of this. I probably won't hear right for a week after the chief yells at me."

Max grabbed a washcloth from the neat stack in the open shelving above the toilet. "Yeah, well. Maybe that will ensure that you remember next time." He wet and soaped up the cloth to scrub the sink.

"Oh, sorry," a feminine voice said. "I didn't know you were still changing."

Max turned around to see Bex backing up from the doorway, a handful of fresh washcloths and towels in her hands. Dillon melted back into the shadows of the hallway, leaving the two of them alone.

"Don't go," Max said. "You can put those up in here. Sorry about the mess I'm making." He plopped the washcloth into the sink and moved back so she could enter the small room.

She hesitated, her gaze falling to his chest, before she cleared her throat and looked away. "No problem. Are you kidding? You saved my life. Again. Make all the messes you want. I didn't remember whether I had enough towels still in here, with all the packing I did. Looks like there are plenty. I'll just put these back in the box—"

"Bex, wait." When she still turned to leave, he added, "Please."

She froze, then turned back toward him, a foot back from the doorway. "Was there something else you needed?"

He let out a deep sigh. "Are you okay?"

"Of course." She absently stroked her fingertips across the bandage on her left forearm. "Like I said, you saved my life. Thank you. That sounds so inadequate. But…thank you."

He braced his hands on the door frame on either side of her. "It can't be easy having someone try to kill you twice in one day. Especially with the two events appearing unrelated."

"Appearing? You think there's a chance that they are related?"

"I didn't say that. Just reserving judgment until we investigate."

"But the shooter, Marcia, she wasn't at the grocery store this morning."

"No. She wasn't."

"Did she say why she tried to shoot me?"

"She collapsed after I cuffed her. They took her to Blount Memorial in Maryville. Probably won't get to interview her until tomorrow. Assuming she doesn't lawyer up by then."

She seemed to ponder that for a moment, biting her lip as she considered all the possibilities.

"Don't think too hard on it," he said. "That's my job. I'll figure this out. Your job is to be careful, stay alert."

"Because someone else might try to kill me today?"

The bitterness and underlying fear in her voice had him automatically reaching for her, wanting to comfort her. But she hurriedly backed up before he could touch her.

He dropped his hand to his side and smiled as if it didn't matter. Because it shouldn't. What the hell had he been thinking to reach for her? Had he really expected that she'd want his touch? She was the one who'd left. She was the one who'd been gone for ten years. If she wanted anything to do with him, she knew where to find him. And she hadn't come back even once. She hadn't called, texted, sent a freaking email. Clearly, that horse had galloped away years ago, never to return. The sooner he got that through his thick skull, the better off he'd be.

"You can't drive home tonight with your windshield blown out. I'll ask the chief to assign someone to watch over you until your car is fixed. They can—"

"Follow me around? How long would it take your boss to tell them to haul me to the station like he's wanted all along? Thanks, but no thanks. I don't want police protection. I'll take my chances on my own."

"You're being stubborn. At least let me call a security company. They could assign bodyguards—"

"I'm fine, Max. Really. In spite of how things seem, I assure you I can and do usually take care of myself."

And then she was gone, taking her armload of towels with her.

Footsteps sounded in the hall and Dillon stuck his head in the door again. "Hey, man. One of the Piggly Wiggly suspects at Blount Memorial is already out of surgery. The chief wants me to head over there to question him the moment he wakes up, preferably before he asks for a lawyer. But Marcia Knolls is at the hospital being checked out, too, and already saying she wants to cut a deal, so I've got my hands full. Everyone else's plate is loaded already. Can you help me out?"

"You bet." Max grabbed his clean shirt and yanked it over his head.

Dillon hesitated. "Could be an all-nighter. You sure you don't want to hang here? With Bex?"

Max stared at him. "You sure you want to ask me that question?"

Dillon held up his hands in a placating gesture. "Hey, I had to ask."

Max glanced at his watch. Almost shift change for the uniformed officers. He grabbed his cell phone out of its holder. "Did I see Jake Cantor outside earlier with the other uniforms?"

"I think so, why?"

"Can you ask him to meet me in the living room on your way out? I need to ask him something."

Dillon gave him a long look, then sighed. "All right. Keep your secrets. I'll send him in. Make it quick though. I'll meet you at my truck." He headed down the hallway.

Max did a quick internet search on his phone. When he found what he was looking for, he made a call, then went into the living room. When he spotted Officer Cantor standing by the fireplace looking impatient, he strode to him.

"Hey, Jake."

"Max. What's up? I was about to head back to the station to finish my reports for the shift change."

After a quick look around to make sure that Bex wasn't within earshot, Max said, "If you don't mind putting that off for a little while, I need your help. I've hired a bodyguard service to keep an eye on Miss Kane. But I need someone to watch over her until their guy gets here. I know you do security work on the side sometimes. I'll pay your fee—"

"No way, man. Keep your money. I can wait until your guy gets here. Not a problem. I take it Miss Kane doesn't know about this?"

"No. And I don't want her to. She sort of has a phobia about the police. Or at least, Destiny police. She refused our protection. So I can't ask the chief to assign anyone."

He looked confused over Bex's distrust of the local police, probably because he wasn't around back when Bobby Caldwell was killed—and the chief threw Bex in jail.

"Okay," Jake said. "This stays on the downlow. Like I said, not a problem. Give your bodyguard my cell number. I saw Miss Kane out on the lawn talking to one of the other detectives a few minutes ago. I'll keep an eye on her until he gets here."

Max shook his hand. "Thanks, Jake. I owe you one. When you talk to this guy, stress again for me that he and his team need to make sure Bex, Miss Kane, doesn't spot them. They need to be invisible."

"You got it."

Chapter Seven

Max shifted in the uncomfortable plastic hospital chair that he'd slept in most of last night. Beside him, lying in bed with one hand cuffed to the railing, was grocery store shooter Lenny Stinsky.

The all-nighter that Dillon had predicted had turned into all night and most of the next day. It was already nearing the dinner hour. But Max wasn't going anywhere, not when his long wait was finally about to pay off. According to Lenny's doctor, he was now healthy enough to talk and awake enough to understand his Miranda rights.

To be absolutely certain of that, to reduce the possibility of Lenny's statement being thrown out at trial, the chief had decided to be in on the interview. Which was why Max was sitting on one side of Lenny's bed while the chief was on the other. But since neither of them was proficient at playing good cop, this was going to be a tag team of bad cop, bad cop. Meaning they were going to lie through their teeth to try to get as much information as they could out of the little tattoo-covered delinquent.

As gangbangers went, Lenny Stinsky was the scrawniest, least tough-looking one that Max had ever seen. Not that he'd seen all that many in Destiny. Mostly he was going by what he'd seen on TV.

The kid was eighteen, just barely. But he looked so small and scared that he could have passed for fifteen.

Luck was definitely on Max and the chief's side today. Because the other guy Max had shot, a guy with a temper as hot as his hair was red, appeared to be the leader of the gunmen. He was far more jaded and too experienced to talk to the cops. He'd asked for a lawyer the second he woke up from the anesthesia. He'd also demanded to see Lenny. To keep him from talking, of course. But no way was Max going to let him get within a hundred feet of their little squealer.

Max scooted his chair closer to the bed and glanced at the chief sitting on the other side before asking his next question.

"So far you haven't told us much, Lenny. We need names. If you want a deal, you need to give us something worth dealing for. Now start over, and this time give us some details."

Lenny's eyes were wide and uncertain as he glanced from Max to the chief and back again. "What kind of deal do I get?"

"Nothing so far. You have to prove you've got something we want before we talk terms." Max glanced at his watch. "I really don't care which one of the five of you I deal with. The first guy to talk is the one we negotiate with. The rest of you can go to prison for the rest of your lives for all I care."

That wasn't true, of course. Three of the five had suffered only mild concussions from being knocked out and were in county lockup, refusing to talk, just like the other guy who'd been shot and was still in the hospital. Lenny was Max's only hope of getting any information anytime soon. But the little scumbag didn't need to know that.

Lenny's Adam's apple bobbed in this throat.

Max checked his watch again. "Time's up. I'm off to talk to one of the other guys."

"Wait." His hand shot up then jerked short, the handcuff rattling against the bed rail. He winced and lowered his arm. "Okay, okay. I'll start from the top. What do you want to know?"

"Who hired you, for starters? All you've told us is some guy approached you and your homies on a corner in Knoxville. What was his name?"

"I don't know."

Max started to stand again.

"Wait, wait. I'm not lying. I really don't know."

The desperation in the kid's voice told Max he was probably telling the truth. Which didn't bode well for their investigation.

He relaxed back in his chair again, settling in for a long interview. "He never gave you a name?"

Lenny shook his head. "No. I never really saw his face, either. It was at night. We were in an alley, goofing around, when he drives up and parks his car at the entrance, blocking us in. Chucky heads over to make him move, but the guy pulls a gun on him."

"Who's Chucky?" Max asked.

Lenny swallowed. "He…he's our leader. Red hair, about six feet tall, freckles."

The other guy Max had shot.

The chief tapped the bed railing to get the kid's attention. "You saw a guy pull a gun but you can't describe him?"

"Didn't say I couldn't describe him, just not his face. The car's headlights were shining toward us. All I could see was his outline, you know? And the gun. The guy was about six feet tall, average weight, not too skinny but not big, either."

Max rolled his eyes. "That describes half the guys I know. What about his hair color?"

"Didn't see it. Told you it was dark, and the headlights were on."

"What about the gun?"

"That's easy. It was just like the ones he gave us for holding up the grocery store."

"An M16?" Max asked.

Lenny shrugged. "Guess so. Never saw one before that night." He mouth curved. "Pretty bad-ass gun."

A chill swept through Max at the delight on the kid's face. For the first time since the interview had begun, he believed he was seeing the real Lenny Stinsky, the gangbanger who had little to no respect for the lives of others.

"What about the car the guy drove?" Max asked. "What kind was it? Did it have a front license plate?"

The kid shrugged again. "It was one of those SUV things, dark color. Didn't see any plates. Like I said, the—"

"Headlights were too bright, yeah, yeah. Did he make the deal with Chucky or all of you?"

"All of us."

"How much?"

"Ten thousand."

Max scoffed. "You risked years of prison time for a split of two thousand dollars?"

Lenny shook his head. "Not a split. Each."

Max shot a look at the chief. "You're saying this guy came out of nowhere and hired the five of you for fifty thousand dollars?"

"Yep." A gloating look crossed Lenny's face, until he tried to cross his arms and couldn't because of the handcuffs. He yanked them against the rail and frowned.

"Did he pay up front?"

"I ain't sayin'."

Code words for he wasn't going to tell the cops where his money was. Max didn't bother going down that tangent. They'd follow the money trail later. What he needed right now was a name.

"What were the exact terms of the deal? Did you hear him? Or did Chucky relay the information?"

"You're kidding, right?" He shook his head like he thought Max was an idiot. "No way was any of us getting near him with that wicked-looking gun. We hung back and waited for Chucky to tell us what the guy said. The guy talked to Chucky, then tossed a duffel bag on the ground and drove off."

Max's stomach sank. The chief was already scrubbing his face and shaking his head. If everything Lenny had just told them was hearsay, they had the legal equivalent of zero in a court of law. And they couldn't base any potential search warrants off hearsay, either. Lenny was looking more and more like a dead end.

"Lenny, I'm going to ask you again. This is really important, so think hard before you answer. Did you personally hear anything the gun-man said?"

"Oh, yeah. Of course."

Max gripped the arms of the chair. "Good, good. What exactly did you hear him say?"

"When Chucky headed toward the guy's car, the man said, 'Hold it right there. I want to make you a deal.' A couple of minutes later the guy was gone and we had the address to that store and a picture of the gal we were supposed to scare." He grinned. "And those sweet M16 rifles."

Max shook his head in disgust. He pushed his chair back and stood. The chief was slower, but he stood, too.

"I did good, right?" Lenny looked back and forth. "We got a deal? I don't do no time?"

Max wrapped his fingers around the foot rail and leaned toward him. "No, Lenny. We ain't got no deal. All you've told me is that you have no direct knowledge of who hired you to storm the Piggly Wiggly and that you can't even describe the guy or give us his name. In other words, you have nothing."

They headed toward the door.

The handcuffs rattled against the bedrail. "Wait, I told you what I know. Where are you going?"

Max let the door swing closed behind him and the chief.

The chief put his hand on his hips. "Which one is Chucky? One of the ones over at county lockup?"

"No. He's the other guy I shot, the one who asked for a lawyer."

"Figures." Thornton motioned with his thumb over his shoulder. "If this Lenny guy told us the truth, the other three gunmen won't be able to help us any more than he did, even if they weren't already asking for lawyers."

"That about sums it up," Max said.

The sound of footsteps coming down the polished tiled hallway had Max turning around, surprised to see Dillon striding toward them.

When Dillon reached them, Max asked, "What are you still doing here? Didn't you get Marcia's statement yesterday? Or did something else happen?"

"No, nothing else, thank goodness. But there was a delay with her statement. The doctors around here are a little too careful, if you ask me. They wouldn't let me talk to her yesterday at all, even though she called us. I had to wait for them to clear her."

"They're terrified of lawsuits these days," the chief grumbled. "Is she ready to talk now?"

"I just finished interviewing her. She answered every question I asked and then some. She's terrified of going to jail. But nothing she said ties into the grocery store holdup. Her going after Miss Kane with that rifle was apparently a spur-of-the-moment decision. Marcia fancies herself Bobby Caldwell's girlfriend and blames Miss Kane for his death. She said when she saw her with you, Max, that all those old feelings of anger came back. She was furious that Max and Bex were back together and she could never be with Bobby again."

"We're not back together," Max gritted out.

Dillon shrugged. "Just relaying what the witness—"

"You mean suspect."

"Fair enough. I'm just telling you what she said. She was jealous and angry and grabbed the rifle out of the trunk of her car. She claims she was only trying to scare Miss Kane."

"Right. And she just happened to have a loaded rifle in her car when she came over."

The chief cleared his throat, drawing their attention. "Not that I want to give Miss Knolls an alibi or reasonable doubt, but she has won the shooting challenges at the county fair three years running. The fair is coming up soon. It's likely she keeps her gun in the car to take back and forth to target practice these days."

Dillon grimaced. "You hit it on the head, Chief.

That's exactly what she told me, that she was going to do some target practice after bringing over a casserole her mom made her deliver to Miss Kane. She also insisted that if she'd really wanted to shoot anyone, she wouldn't have missed."

The chief nodded.

"Please don't tell me you agree with that statement," Max said.

"Okay. I'll just keep quiet, then." The chief rolled his eyes.

Max swore. "So we have her on, what, a misdemeanor? Assuming we believe her story?"

"Well." The chief scrubbed the stubble on his chin. "We could charge her with attempted murder if we wanted to go that route. But a jury of her peers would set her free so fast your head would spin. Trying to pin the grocery store thing on her won't stick, either."

"Then you're just going to let her go? I don't care how proficient she is with a rifle. No one's perfect. She could have hurt or killed Bex when she pulled that trigger."

"I ain't gonna argue with you on that," the chief agreed. "We'll charge her with something, maybe reckless endangerment. Let her spend a few nights in jail to teach her a lesson. But unless

Miss Kane wants to press more serious charges against her, she'll be out in a few days."

Max whirled around and headed down the hallway.

"Where are you going?" the chief called out.

"To get Bex to press charges against Marcia Knolls."

Chapter Eight

Bex parked her mom's ancient Ford Taurus in front of her lawyer's office and cut the engine. She would have much preferred to take her own, far newer SUV, but until she could get the windshield replaced, the Taurus would have to do. Hopefully she could get her car fixed soon and get out of town. It was as if the universe was against her, throwing obstacles in her path to keep her from leaving.

Just this morning, she'd come across more of her mom's things packed in the attic. And she'd spent most of the day sorting through them and figuring out where to take them. It wasn't like she could throw away homemade quilts and other keepsakes her mom had collected over the years. But Bex didn't have room in her condo to hoard everything, either. So she'd kept the more sentimental of the items and spent hours driving around Destiny delivering the rest of them to longtime friends of her mother.

That had taken even more time, of course, since she couldn't just walk up, leave her mom's things, and not stay and visit. That kind of rudeness would have made her mother ashamed to call her daughter. So she'd done her duty, answering her mom's friends' questions about what she'd been doing all these years. Telling them about the antique store she ran with her best friend in Knoxville, building a comfortable life for herself, if not an exciting one.

The close-knit group had known about her, of course. They'd known that her mother visited Bex several times a year. They also knew that her mom had forbidden Bex to come to Destiny because she was so worried about the shadow of her past hanging over her head.

Her mom had been nothing if not protective. And her friends had served her well, keeping her secret until the very end. They were also steadfast in their support of Bex, flat out telling her they knew she was innocent, that she hadn't killed that stalker-boy. Their support had Bex so close to tears she'd almost broken down in front of them.

Now she was finally alone once again, back in town with another task to finish. But even though she was anxious to be done, she hesitated to get out of the car. Glancing in the rearview mirror at the grocery store across the street sent a chill of dread racing up her spine.

She'd been so lucky to have escaped not one but two shootings without serious injury. But she couldn't count on Max always being there to protect her. Bad things came in threes, didn't they? Her mom's death had been the first terrible blow. Hopefully the two shootings counted as the second and third bad things and nothing else would happen before she could escape this town again.

She shoved the door open and headed into the two-story office building. The exterior door opened onto a short hall with a bench and another door at the end that she knew from previous visits was the bathroom. She stepped past the bench and through the open doorway into the reception area.

Her attorney's assistant looked up from some papers on her desk and gave Bex a brilliant smile, as she did with everyone.

"Miss Kane, so nice to see you again. Are you here to make an appointment?"

Bex smiled at the elderly woman who was just as perfectly put together as her dapper employer. Martha couldn't be a day younger than seventy, but she got around just as well as women half her age and looked like she could have graced the pages of a fashion magazine. Bex had loved the kind woman the moment she'd met her and always felt lighter in spirit after talking to her.

"Hi, Martha. It's good to see you, too. I don't have an appointment, but Mr. Leonard said I could stop by anytime to sign a power of attorney."

"Oh, sure. Of course. I can take care of that for you. No appointment needed. Good thing, too. Because he's got someone in his office right now. I wouldn't want you to have to wait. Have a seat while I get the form." She waved toward the row of cushy leather chairs against the wall across from her desk.

Bex murmured her thanks and settled into one of the chairs as Martha headed down a hallway behind her desk to what Bex assumed was a storage room. The building was small, housing the one-lawyer office downstairs and living quarters for Mr. Leonard upstairs.

She glanced to her right at the closed door to her lawyer's office. She would have liked to tell him goodbye before leaving town. But even if she had to wait another day for her windshield to get repaired before she returned to Knoxville, she doubted she'd come back to her lawyer's office before then. In town, she felt too exposed, vulnerable.

Max's warnings, his encouragement for her to let the chief assign someone to protect her hadn't fallen on deaf ears. The only reason she'd refused the offer was because she didn't trust the chief, or any of the Destiny police, except Max. And he hadn't exactly jumped at the chance to be the one to protect her.

Max. Just thinking about him had her chest hurting again. Would he be happy once she was gone so he could get on with his life again, without her interference? Without her bringing up memories he'd much rather forget?

Leaving would make it more difficult for him to conduct his investigations into the shootings. But other than that, would he miss her? The idea seemed ludicrous given that every conversation they'd had was fraught with tension and anger. All she knew for sure was that she would miss him. Or maybe it was the idea of him—the way they'd been as a couple. Bex and Max, always together, so much so that friends had taken to calling them Mex—which she hated but that Max had thought was funny. So funny that he'd teased her that they should move to Texas someday and be Tex Mex.

It was amazing how quickly the years could melt away after seeing someone again. She wondered how long it would take before she could go a whole day without thinking about him. It had taken years to get to that point the last time. She didn't imagine it would be any easier this time.

He wasn't the kind of man a woman could easily forget.

The click of sensible heels on hardwood floors heralded Martha's return. With clipboard in hand, she crossed the room before Bex could climb out of the chair she'd sunk into.

Martha waved her to stay seated. "No need to get up. I know how those chairs are. They grab you and hold on. Augustus needs to put something harder and less comfortable in here." She handed the clipboard and a pen to Bex. "You can read over this and fill it out right there. As soon as you're done, I'll make sure you signed everywhere you needed to sign and then I'll notarize it and give you a copy. Take your time."

Bex thanked her again and read through the form. Everything seemed straightforward. She initialed a couple of paragraphs where Martha had marked an X and then signed the bottom. Now to climb out of the person-eating chair. She set the clipboard on the little table beside her and grasped the arms of the chair.

Suddenly a large, familiar tanned hand appeared in front of her to help her up. She selfishly allowed her gaze to travel up him a bit more slowly than she should, enjoying every little piece of scenery the trip revealed—from his narrow jeans-clad hips with the oversize rodeo-style belt buckle to his flat waist, the soft-looking forest green shirt that revealed a small dark matting of hair at the V of his neck. But no matter how much she tried to prepare herself for the final destination, her breath still caught when she viewed his handsome, angular face and those amazing warm brown eyes that seemed to tug at her very soul whenever he looked at her.

One of his dark brows arched and a smile tugged at the corner of his mouth. "You okay, Bex? You seem a little preoccupied."

She put her hand in his, savoring the warm feel of his skin against hers as he effortlessly tugged her out of the chair. And loving that he seemed in a better mood today, gifting her with a smile.

"I was just thinking it was about time you showed up," she teased, feeling happier for some reason.

"You were expecting me?"

She reluctantly pulled her hand from his and smoothed her blouse over her khaki pants. "I'm getting used to you saving me. And I'm pretty sure my life was in danger in that chair."

His smile widened. "I've heard small children have disappeared in those monster chairs." He glanced around, nodded at Martha. "I thought I might find you here. When you're done, maybe I can take you to Eva-Marie's for dinner. I want to update you on a few developments. And maybe if I ply you with some of Eva's homemade pecan pie, I can convince you to work through your fear of the police station and come in to give a formal statement."

Her ridiculous happiness at seeing him faded and she shook her head. "I'm not ever going back there."

He cocked his head, as if he was sizing her up, planning strategies. "I want to make sure you're safe, Bex."

"I'm not taking any foolish chances. I'm going home as soon as feasible."

"Not to Pigeon Forge to relax a few weeks first?"

She shook her head. "No. I've…decided to go straight to Knoxville." Because now she realized that if she went to Pigeon Forge all she'd do was think of Max and the last time they'd been there. And that wasn't something she could handle right now.

"How about we have dinner and talk about your plans, and your safety? Plus, I need to talk to you about Marcia Knolls."

She shouldn't say yes. And she really didn't want to discuss anything to do with Marcia. But she heard herself saying, "You buying?"

"Of course."

"Okay. I'll join you, but only because I'm too financially savvy to pass up a free meal. And the bagel I had this morning has long since lost its ability to stave off the growling in my stomach. But don't expect any miracles. I'm telling you right now that nothing will make me agree to go downtown with you."

"Downtown? You make it sound like we're a big city. You've been gone way too long."

The reason for her being gone seemed to hang like a heavy cloud over both of them, making his smile fade and her body tense. The surprisingly easy camaraderie that had flowed between them a moment ago evaporated, leaving them both on edge and uncomfortable once again. She hated that this was how things were between them. But there wasn't anything that could be done about it.

Bex crossed to the desk and handed Martha the clipboard and pen. "You can mail me a copy later. No rush."

"Oh, nonsense. It'll only take a minute for me to notarize this and make you a copy. I'll be right back."

Bex was about to protest, but Martha was already heading down the hallway behind her desk again.

Max crossed his arms and rocked back on his boots. "I didn't see your RAV4 out front. Is it at Eddie's?"

Eddie's Auto Barn. Bex smiled ruefully. "That place is still around?"

"Yep. Ralph Putnam bought it from Eric Green last year."

"Has anyone ever figured out who the original Eddie was who started the garage?"

"Not as far as I know."

She smiled and felt a tug of nostalgia for the happy years she'd spent growing up here. "Maybe I'll ask Ralph to pick up my car and repair the windshield. I'm driving my mom's Taurus right now and haven't had a chance to put the RAV4 in anywhere to be fixed."

The phone in his pocket buzzed and he pulled it out. He tilted it to see the screen, then frowned. "I've got to take this. Be right back."

She nodded and he headed through the open doorway into the little hallway just outside. Feeling restless, Bex toured the reception area, walking the perimeter of the small room and studying the surprisingly nice artwork. She wondered whether a local painter had created it and leaned closer to look at the signature.

"No, she refused to come to the station. I don't think I can convince her, either."

She straightened, realizing she was unwittingly eavesdropping on Max's phone conversation out in the hall. She was about to move away when he said something else.

"You're changing your mind now? You're the one who ordered me to talk to her in the first place. I'm telling you it's all ancient history with us. We were kids. It meant nothing. Our past isn't why she's refusing to go. It's her past, the Caldwell thing."

She sucked in a breath, his words cutting through her like knives.

Ancient history.

It meant nothing.

"You like that painting? My oldest grand-daughter did that."

Bex turned around to see Martha standing behind her desk, papers in her hand, a proud smile on her face.

"Um, yes. It's quite lovely." She hurriedly moved away from the doorway toward the desk.

Footsteps sounded behind her, and she knew Max had entered the room again. She glanced at him and caught him frowning. He looked at the painting by the doorway, then her. Had he heard Martha talking to her? Did he suspect she'd over-heard his call?

He looked like he was about to say something when the door to Mr. Leonard's office opened behind him, letting the sound of several male voices into the room. A wheelchair came into view first, and Bex frowned in surprise to see Robert Caldwell sitting there. The last time she'd seen him he'd been a strong bear of a man. Now he was pale, thin and sickly. Had losing his oldest son done that to him? She pressed a hand against her throat, feeling a stab of nausea at the thought. And then she looked up at the man pushing the wheelchair and took a quick step back.

"Bex?" Max whispered. "What's wrong?"

She blinked at the apparition in front of her. Bobby Caldwell. It couldn't be. How was this possible?

"Bex?" Max moved in front of her, bending down so their eyes met. "Pull yourself together," he whispered.

"But how can it be? Bobby is…" She worked her mouth but couldn't seem to say it out loud, that Bobby was supposed to be dead.

His brows raised and a look of dawning came over his face. "That's Deacon, just back from a tour overseas, Iraq. He's Bobby's younger brother. Remember how much alike they always looked? I assure you that Bobby Caldwell hasn't come back from the grave."

She let out a shaky breath and nodded. "Yes, of course. It was just…a surprise. I'm fine." At his skeptical look, she straightened her shoulders. "I'm fine. Really."

He stepped back beside her. But she almost wished he hadn't. Because now the elder Caldwell had a clear view of her, and his eyes were filled with such hate that it had her stomach churning with nausea all over again. His face reddened and his eyes darkened almost to black.

Mr. Leonard, seemingly unaware of the tension in the room, stepped around the Caldwells to greet Bex. He took her hands in his. "Delighted to see you again, dear. Are you here to sign that form?"

"Um, yes. Martha already had me sign it. I was just about to leave. I didn't mean to intrude." She tugged her hands from his.

"Nonsense, nonsense," he said. "No need to rush." He nodded at Max. "Good to see you, Detective. I hope everything's okay? No other crises happening in our little town?"

Max shook his hand. "So far, so good." He stepped past the lawyer and shook Deacon's hand. "Deacon, good to see you. Thank you for your service. Glad to see you made it back in one piece."

"Thanks, Max. Good to be back." Deacon shook his hand.

Max nodded at the man in the wheelchair. "Mr. Caldwell."

"What's she doing here?" The older man's words dripped like venom from his mouth.

Bex curled her fingers into her palms.

Mr. Leonard turned around, his face mirroring surprise for a split second. Then a look of dawning came over him. He gave Bex an apologetic glance before facing his other clients.

"Robert, I'll have those papers drawn up in no time. Have Deacon bring you back in a week and we'll perform a final review."

Relief flashed in Deacon's eyes and he started forward, pushing his father's chair and looking eager to escape.

"Hold it," his father demanded, slamming one of the brakes on the wheelchair and almost overturning it in his zeal to stop. "I'm not going anywhere until I hear an explanation for why she's here. Augustus, if you're going to do business with this murdering piece of vermin, I'll take my business elsewhere."

Bex sucked in a breath, and Deacon's mouth fell open in astonishment.

Mr. Leonard sputtered and stammered, seemingly so shocked that he didn't know what to say.

Max had no such problem. He planted himself squarely in front of the elder Caldwell's chair and leaned down, both hands braced on the arms of the wheelchair.

"Calling Miss Kane a murderer is slander, Mr. Caldwell. And Destiny is just old-fashioned enough to still have laws on the books that give me the power to arrest you for that. I suggest you keep your insults to yourself unless you want to see the inside of a jail cell."

"Bah, Thornton would toss you out on your backside if you put one hand on me. And it's not slander if it's true. That, that—"

"Careful," Max warned, his eyes narrowed dangerously.

Caldwell glared at him before aiming his fury at Bex again. "You killed my son. You shouldn't be free and walking around. You should be six feet under, just like him."

"Dad." Deacon sounded mortified. "Please, stop." He aimed a pleading look at Bex. "I'm so sorry, Bex. It's the cancer. He doesn't know what he's saying."

"The hell I don't. Stop making excuses for me, you dolt. You never did have the sense your brother had."

Deacon winced and shot Bex another pleading look, as if begging her to overlook his father's poor manners.

Bex was shaking too hard to say anything, so she simply tipped her head at Deacon, trying to let him know that she didn't hold his father's enmity against him.

Max leaned down and said something beneath his breath to the older man. Then he motioned to Deacon. "Get him out of here before I make good on my threat to arrest him."

Deacon flipped the brake and quickly wheeled his father out the door. The old man didn't say anything else to Bex, but his hatred and fury were clear as his glare followed her until the door closed behind the two of them.

Silence reigned inside the little office. Max looked like he wanted to shoot someone. Martha looked horrified, papers dangling from her fingertips. And Mr. Leonard appeared equally nonplussed, his mouth opening and closing as if he wasn't sure what to say.

Bex cleared her throat and ran a shaky hand through her hair, flipping the long strands back over her shoulder. "I'd better go. Thank you for your help this week, Mr. Leonard." She stepped toward Martha and held out her hand. "Is one of those for me?"

Martha blinked, then looked down at the papers. "Oh, yes, my apologies. Here you go." She held one of the papers out to Bex, her smile decidedly less bright this time.

"Thank you." Bex turned and hurried toward the door. It opened just as she reached it. Max was holding the door. "Thanks," she whispered, barely able to force even one more word past her tight throat.

When they were outside, she hurried to the Taurus and opened the driver's door.

"Bex." Max's deep voice sounded behind her.

She cleared her throat but didn't turn to face him. She didn't want him to see how hard she was struggling not to cry. Because she wasn't this weak woman who cried every time something didn't go her way. Until she'd seen Max again after all these years.

"Sorry about dinner," she said. "I'm not hungry anymore."

"Bex, wait. Please. I need to explain—"

She slid into the driver's seat and shut the door to block whatever he was saying. The tears were flowing freely now. All she could hope was that the angle of the car and the tint on the windshield kept him from seeing that she was crying.

She dashed her tears away and a few moments later she was driving down the road, just like ten years ago, with Destiny, and Max, in her rearview mirror.

Chapter Nine

It was tempting to barrel down the highway to Knoxville and pretend none of this had ever happened. But Bex rather doubted her mother's old car would make it. And she was too mentally exhausted right now to make that trip.

But she wasn't quite ready to return to her mother's house, either. She was far too upset, and seeing the empty house wasn't going to make her feel any better. So, instead, she wound aimlessly down the backroads until the sun began to sink in the sky, going nowhere in particular, trying to drive out her frustrations.

Driving on gravel roads was apparently a skill she'd forgotten long ago. She was forced to slow down almost to a crawl to keep her car from sliding on the loose rocks and ending up in a ditch.

It suddenly dawned on her where she was, and what was close by. She'd never intended to drive down this particular road. But now that she was here, it seemed that fate had raised its hand. And she started looking in earnest for the turnoff she knew had to be close by.

It didn't help that the road was overgrown with weeds, the edges hard to see, especially in the gloom from the oak tree branches blocking out the fading sunlight overhead. Maybe she should turn around and rent a four-wheel drive before coming out here. Then again, if she didn't do this now, she never would.

She wasn't sure why doing this was suddenly so important. After all, living in the past had never done anything for her before. But with the present so painful, maybe this was just the thing, to remember better times and pretend, if only for a moment, that all the bad had never happened.

"Where are you, where are you?" she muttered, peering through the trees on the right side of the road. Just when she thought she'd have to give up and turn around, she saw it—an old, weathered barn hundreds of yards away, perched upon a slight rise.

She slowed the Taurus, mildly surprised she was able to make the turnoff without wrecking the ancient car. The trees fell away as she accelerated across the fallow field, dried-up remnants of cornstalks, long since harvested, the only evidence of the last crop that had been planted here.

In her mind's eye, the barn was like a familiar

Norman Rockwell painting, a beacon of happier times, welcoming her home. But she couldn't ignore reality for long. The barn was dilapidated, crouching like an evil gargoyle against the dead land surrounding it. Time had not been kind to the abandoned building. Holes had been punched in its rotten walls, probably by animals that had made their homes inside. She parked beside it, not too close, for fear a stiff breeze might blow the building over on top of her car.

Leaving her purse and keys in the Taurus, she made a slow circuit around to the front of the barn and stopped. Funny how so much had changed, and yet, everything was the same. The red paint that had once graced the structure was nearly gone. But the initials carved into one of the boards to the right of the door remained— MR + BK, with a Cupid's arrow running through the middle.

Max's words at the lawyer's office echoed in her mind.

Ancient history. It meant nothing.

That last part was what hurt the most. *It meant nothing.* What had he meant by "it"? The seven years they'd been best friends? The three years they'd been serious boyfriend and girlfriend? That last year, when they'd finally gone all the way? They'd pledged their love to each other. Had it all been a lie on Max's part? Had everything he'd said in her mother's kitchen been a ploy to get her to talk?

It shouldn't matter. Good grief, she was approaching thirty now. A small-business owner with an established life in another town, with friends who didn't care about whatever past she'd left behind. This barn, those initials carved in the wood, they were the part of her life that really *was* ancient history, just as Max had said.

But it was *her* history, a very important part that had made her the person she was today, for better or for worse. And she'd never realized until now just how stuck in the past she was, and that she'd never really cut the tether to Destiny. To Max. Part of her was still here. Part of her had never left.

Until now, she'd never wondered whether the love between her and Max had been real or not. Just thinking that what she'd thought of as the very best part of her life, as a beautiful experience, might have meant nothing to him twisted a knife deeper into her heart.

Angrily brushing at the tears running down her cheeks again, she sent up a quick prayer that the building was sturdier than it looked and headed toward the enormous double doors built to accommodate a small tractor, or maybe a pair of draft horses in older times.

The rusty chain looped from one door handle

to the other was more of a suggestion than an impediment to her getting inside. All she had to do was squeeze in the opening between the two doors after ducking beneath the chain. And suddenly it was ten years ago, as if she'd never left.

The missing and damaged boards allowed enough light to seep in for her to see that little had changed inside since she and Max had sneaked into this old barn that first night, and again several more times after that. He'd laid a blanket and pillow down onto a bed of fresh hay. They'd introduced each other to a world of passion that neither of them had ever experienced before. It was the most wonderful moment of her young life up to that point. She'd been so naive, believing that love would last forever. But nothing lasted forever, if indeed it had ever existed.

She wrapped her arms around her waist and stepped farther into the barn.

"What are you doing in here, Bex? It's dangerous. Didn't you see the No Trespassing signs out front?"

She whirled around, pressing a hand against her heart even as she recognized Max's voice.

His eyes narrowed as he stepped closer. "You've been crying."

"I'm fine. What are you doing here? This can't be a coincidence."

"I tailed you out of town." He held up his hands

as if to stop any angry words. "I wasn't trying to be intrusive or nosy. But you seemed upset and I was worried about you driving while upset. I just wanted to make sure you got home okay." He looked around the barn. "Imagine my surprise when you turned in here."

She wasn't feeling charitable enough at the moment to believe that he'd followed her out of worry. In fact, she was more inclined to believe something else entirely.

"I didn't wreck. Yay me. But I'm thinking your true reason for following me is that your chief ordered you to. Well, you can turn around and go back to the station. Tell him you did your duty, tried once again to convince me to go to the station, and once again I refused. Go on. I don't need you here. And we both know you sure as hell don't want to be here. Not with me. If you ever did."

She turned her back on him and waited to hear his boots make a path to the doors. Instead, he moved closer. She could feel the heat of his body at her back even through her sweater. And she hated that what she wanted to do, what she really craved, was to take one step back and lean into him. She wanted to feel his arms come down around her, hold her and this time never let her go. And she hated herself for it.

"Bex, what's wrong?" His deep voice curled itself around her like an invitation.

It was insane that being this close to him could have such an impact on her. He was setting her on fire, making her body yearn for him, as if it remembered him and ached to be with him again. How could she want him when she hurt so much inside and her mind was screaming at her that she was a fool?

She didn't answer, couldn't answer, without revealing the war going on inside her.

His heavy sigh seemed loud in the quiet barn. "How long are you going to stand there? What did you plan on doing when you came in here?"

She shrugged. Let him think she was being difficult instead of that she was paralyzed by her own traitorous emotions. If he touched her right now, she knew she wouldn't be able to walk away. Perhaps it was the emotional roller coaster she'd been on since getting that shocking call that her mother had passed unexpectedly that made her so vulnerable. Maybe it was coming so close to death herself that had her yearning for what she'd once had but could never have again. A sob built in her throat. She ruthlessly held it back, clenching her hands into fists at her side.

Go away, Max. Can't you see you're killing me?

"At least let me escort you back to your mom's."

The confusion and irritation in his voice was exactly what she'd needed. It helped her snap out of her pity party and gave her enough of a flash of irritation at him to finally speak.

"No, thank you. I'm not ready to go back."

There. That had sounded strong, unaffected, confident. Hadn't it? Surely he hadn't heard the little wobble in her voice. It had only been a tiny little wobble.

"Bex?" His voice was softer this time. "Are you all right?"

She squeezed her eyes shut, drew two deep, bracing breaths. "Just go, okay? You don't owe me anything. It's not like we're in a relationship anymore."

Her voice was thick with tears, but there was nothing she could do about it. She just needed him to stop torturing her and leave before she melted into a puddle of misery. His hurtful words from back in town poured out of her in a sea of bitterness. "Whatever happened in the past was ancient history anyway. Didn't even matter."

"I knew it. I knew you heard that stupid phone call." He turned her around and put his hand beneath her chin, forcing her to look at him. "I'm sorry, Bex. I was a jerk back there, okay?"

"Back where? At the grocery store deli, when you ignored me? Or the lawyer's office, where you basically told your boss—or whoever was on the phone—that I wasn't even a blip on your life's radar? I'm guessing when we made love here that never mattered, either." Tears ran down her cheeks and she swiped them away. She swore. "I did *not* come here for this. I don't want to do this. Please, Max. Just go."

He grabbed her shoulders, his eyes dark with anger and frustration. "You're the one who turned down my proposal. You're the one who left. So why are you so angry at me?"

She shook her head, her throat tight.

He started to say something else, then stopped. Started again, then swore and yanked her against him. He wanted to kiss her. She could see it in the way his mouth tightened, the way his gaze dropped to her lips. And for one crazy minute, she wanted the same thing. She wanted his mouth swooping down on hers, consuming her in a wild, angry kiss that was nothing like the tender kisses they'd shared as teenagers. She wanted—needed—crazy right now. A kiss so unexpected and incredibly hot that they'd both be panting by the time they broke apart.

She blinked up at him, her shaking fingers pressing against her lips. Just the thought of him kissing her had her mouth tingling.

His nostrils flared as he watched her fingers. Then he shook his head, as if trying to clear his mind. And the moment, the spell, whatever it was, was gone. But the anger, the hurt, wasn't.

"Just because I don't want to share every intimate detail of my life with my boss doesn't mean our past was a lie. It meant something, Bex," he rasped, his voice ragged. "*We* meant something."

And then he was gone.

She didn't know how long she stood there, his words repeating themselves over and over in her mind, confusing her even more than she was before.

We meant something.

She stood there for a long time, until the shadows began to lengthen, until a noise in the loft spooked her and she berated herself for being silly. No telling what kinds of animals made their home here in this old, abandoned barn.

She slipped between the chains and headed to the Taurus. She'd just started to circle back toward the road when something in her rearview mirror had her slamming on the brakes. She stared long and hard at the mirror, which showed the front of the barn. But several minutes passed and she didn't see anything else.

Laughing nervously, she told herself her mind was playing tricks on her. The roof overhang must have cast a shadow across the doors to make it look like a man had slipped through the chains and run around the side of the building.

Chapter Ten

After wolfing down a hearty breakfast of bacon, eggs, biscuits and gravy at Eva-Marie's diner, Max leaned back against the corner booth. And settled in to wait.

He glanced at his watch, then at the door to the diner, dreading the upcoming conversation. He still wasn't sure why he was doing this. Then again, who was he kidding? He was doing this because of what had happened last night with Bex, or, what had *almost* happened. And how badly he'd wanted it to happen.

That alone, the fact that it had nearly killed him not to kiss her, told him that this meeting he'd set up this morning was the right thing to do. The honorable thing to do. Even though he had no intention of pursuing a relationship with Bex again. Thoughts of her were consuming his days, his nights, no matter how hard he tried to push them out of his head. And that made it impossible, and wrong, to remain in a relationship with someone else. It was time to end his three-week dating spree with police intern Monica Stevens.

Breaking up with someone in a diner made him cringe. He'd tried to schedule this discussion at her place, or his. But as soon as he'd called her this morning, saying they needed to talk, it was as if her sixth sense had kicked in. She'd become distant, defensive, and insisted that they meet here. In public. Why she wanted to do that, he had no idea.

Then again, as the door opened and she strutted inside, he realized exactly why she'd chosen this particular place. He'd wanted to spare her feelings and not make a scene. But she obviously had no such intentions toward him.

Monica strode down the center aisle, her heavily made-up eyes tracking him like a radar-guided missile. Her long, blond hair bounced around her shoulders. Impossibly tight jeans outlined her curvy figure, tapering down her long legs to a pair of bloodred stilettos that clicked across the black-and-white tiled floor. Every head turned her way, watching her deliberate progress until she stopped beside Max's booth.

He started to stand but she waved him back down.

"Don't bother acting the gentleman now." She put her hands on her hips. "You think I don't know what you're doing? This whole town is talking about your little girlfriend and how you carried her out of the grocery store all lovey-dovey." She rolled her eyes. "Now you're breaking up with me so you can go screw that boyfriend-stealer again. Admit it."

A gasp of outrage sounded behind her. Monica looked over her shoulder to see Sally, the waitress, holding a pot of coffee, her mouth hanging open.

"Go away." Monica made a shooing motion with her hand. "We're busy."

Max shot Sally an apologetic look before rising to his feet. "I'm sorry."

Monica rolled her eyes again. "It's a little late for that."

"I was talking to Sally."

Monica narrowed her eyes.

Sally glared at Monica's back and whirled around.

Max tossed some bills onto the table. "Let's go somewhere private."

Her hands went back to her hips. "Are you breaking up with me or not?"

He didn't have to look past her to know that everyone was listening for his response. She'd practically yelled her question. And the place had gone completely silent.

"Monica—"

"Answer me," she shouted.

He winced. "We've only been dating for a few weeks. I hardly think it qualifies as a breakup. But, yes, I've got a lot of things going on with the investigation and all. You deserve someone who can focus on you and right now that's not me. I think we should stop seeing each other—"

Whap!

Her hand slapped his cheek. The sting was nothing compared to the sting to his pride as she pivoted on her stilettos and marched out of the diner. He'd never made a woman angry enough to slap him before, and it bothered him that he'd done so now.

"Good riddance is all I can say." Sally stopped in front of him and refilled his coffee cup. "I could tell she was trouble from the minute the chief hired her. You never should've taken up with the likes of her."

Max sat back down, figuring another cup of coffee might do him some good. Since Sally was still standing there, expecting a reply, he shrugged.

"She's an intelligent, nice woman. I can't blame her for being upset. As soon as I knew that Bex was back in town I should have told Monica about our past. Obviously she heard the rumors from someone else. That had to embarrass her."

"Right. When would you have talked to her?

After the first shooting or the second?" She shook her head in disgust. "The woman was a police intern, for goodness' sake. She had to know you were busy with the investigations and didn't have time to coddle her. Not that you should anyway." She looked past him, out the window, and her mouth quirked up in a smile. "You been wasting years on types like that Monica woman. When all along you should have been spending time with someone of quality, like her."

She waved toward the window, then took her coffeepot with her as she headed to the counter.

Max looked out at the parking lot, worried that Sally might be trying to fix him up with someone. Then he saw her. Bex. She'd just parked her mom's Taurus in the only space left at the end of the packed lot and was heading toward the diner.

A quick glance at the street confirmed that one of the bodyguards that he'd hired to keep an eye on her was sitting in his car at the curb. He must have seen Max's truck outside and figured she'd be safe inside.

About five inches shorter than Monica, without the stilettos, Bex had lush, dark-brown hair that fell just past her shoulders. And even though he couldn't see them this far away, he knew her eyes were an incredible sky blue that could darken like a storm whenever she was mad. Or when she was writhing beneath him in passion.

He frowned and shoved that dangerous memory far away. It wouldn't do to dwell on the past. He'd done enough of that yesterday. Seeing her go into that barn where they'd first made love had brought up all kinds of memories he didn't want to deal with again. He'd thought they'd been locked away somewhere tight all this time, or were gone altogether. And yet it had only taken one trip to a ramshackle barn to bring them all back again.

Who was he kidding?

Those feelings had been dredged up the moment he'd seen her standing at the deli counter at the Piggly Wiggly, her dark hair reaching past her shoulders. When he'd rounded the end of the aisle, the shock of seeing her had nearly driven him to his knees. But even though his mind ordered him to stop, turn around, get out of the store before she saw him, his body had other ideas.

His legs had continued to carry him forward like a starving man drawn to an incredible bounty that would either save him or destroy him. He'd been fighting his insane attraction to her ever since. And when he'd followed her into the barn, heard the tears in her voice, the hurt that he'd caused, he'd been lost. He hadn't wanted to leave her there. He hadn't been lying when he said he was worried about her. But at the same time, he knew that if he'd stood there even a second more, he'd have dragged her to the ground and made love to her.

He scrubbed his jaw and shoved the coffee cup away just as Bex walked inside. And just like when Monica had come in earlier, everyone looked to the front. But unlike earlier, Bex's entrance was met with greetings and smiles and a few hugs. There might be a cloud over her in most parts of town, but the old-timers in this diner seemed to have no concerns about Bex's past and whether she was guilty of murder. They were greeting her like old friends, or at least, friends of her mother. It was mostly retired folks in here this time of day. The younger crowd was busy making a living.

When Bex reached his booth, he rose and tipped his head.

"Morning, Bex. Everything okay?"

"Just peachy. Except that strange men I don't know seem to be following me everywhere." Unlike her predecessor, she kept her voice low so it didn't carry to the other tables. And the rest of the patrons had turned around to offer them privacy.

"Strange men?" he asked, glancing around.

She waved toward the car parked at the curb. "I assume you hired him to keep an eye on me."

He let out a deep sigh. So much for the bodyguards being invisible. "Guilty." He studied her a moment. "You don't seem angry." He waved her into the booth and sat across from her.

She shrugged. "Honestly, I was kind of surprised at how easily you backed down when I insisted that I didn't want anyone keeping an eye on me. I felt pretty silly later for not taking you up on your offer and was going to call someone myself when I spotted one of the men outside my house last night. From his mannerisms, I kind of figured he might be a security guy. But I called the police just to be sure."

Max waved Sally over, who came bearing a pot of coffee and an extra cup for Bex, along with a menu.

"Thanks, Sally." Bex smiled. "I appreciate the coffee but I'm really not hungry."

"Let me know if you change your mind." Sally hurried to another table to refill their cups.

"I'm surprised I didn't hear about the call," Max said. "What happened?"

She ruined her coffee with a liberal amount of cream and sugar. "A uniformed officer came over and checked the guy out, then told me he was a bodyguard of all things. But the guy wouldn't say who'd hired him. I let it drop, said not to worry about it, that I was pretty sure who was behind him being there. Thanks, Max. I do appreciate you making sure that I'm safe. Especially since my shadow isn't a cop."

"Ouch."

She winced. "Sorry. No offense. I don't hold it against you that you're a police officer."

He smiled. "Gee. Thanks. I feel so much better now."

She smiled back, then her smile faded. "I can reimburse you for whatever costs—"

"No."

She sighed. "I figured you'd say that. If you change your mind—"

"I won't."

"As stubborn as ever I see," she said.

"One of the many things we have in common."

Her bubble of laughter had several people looking at them, smiling as well, before returning to their meals. He couldn't help smiling, too. Seeing Bex looking happy was too contagious not to have him feeling lighter inside. Her eyes danced with merriment and it was as if all the years between them had never passed. This was the Bex he remembered, the Bex he'd loved.

"What are you thinking about?" he asked.

"You. And me. And Mr. Youngblood's orchard."

He grimaced. "Before or after I thought I could outrun that bull to get you some apples?"

"Oh, definitely after." She laughed. "I warned you not to try it. But you were too stubborn. Once you got an idea in your head you wouldn't let it go. Maybe you should have gone out for the track team. I swear I never saw a human being run that fast."

"Not fast enough."

"You were faster than the bull," she argued.

"But not faster than Mr. Youngblood's buckshot." He winced again, barely refraining from rubbing his posterior at the memory. "I couldn't sit up for a month."

"True." She rested her chin on her palm, a faraway look in her misty blue eyes. "But we had a lot of fun that month. I must have read you over twenty books while you were convalescing."

"You tortured me. At least three of them were romance novels. I've never lived that down with my brothers." He leaned toward her conspiratorially. "I still have to pay them hush money to this day."

"You wouldn't have to pay if you didn't actually like them. Admit it. You've probably got a romance novel under your pillow right now and you read it every night."

He laughed. "I guess you'd have to come over to my place to find out."

Her smile faded, and the easy camaraderie that had sprung up between them evaporated. He wanted to kick himself for getting carried away and destroying the light atmosphere.

They both straightened, and she awkwardly cleared her throat.

"Where do you live anyway?" she asked, before taking a sip of coffee.

"I built a house on some land adjacent to my father's farm. Close enough to keep in touch but far enough away that I've got my privacy."

She nodded, then shoved her cup out of the way.

"I didn't mean to take up so much of your time. I know you're really busy with the investigation. Actually, that's the reason I'm here. I drove into town to take care of a few more errands and when I passed the grocery store I couldn't help thinking about what happened. That's when I remembered something that I didn't tell anyone before. I pulled over to call you when I saw your truck over here in the lot, so I decided to come tell you in person."

"Tell me what?"

"A name. When I was in the grocery store, hiding from the gunmen, I overheard one of them in the next aisle saying something about Reggie telling them that *she* was heading toward the front of the store. I'm not sure what they were talking about. But I figured this Reggie person might be someone who works at the store. And if that's the case—"

"Then there's an insider who might have helped the gunmen."

"Exactly. What do you think? Could that be helpful?"

"It's a lead to follow. Could very well be a great lead. Thanks, Bex."

"Of course. If I think of anything else, I'll let you know." She shoved out of the booth and stood.

Max stood, too. "You seem to be in a hurry."

She hesitated, her gaze dropping from his. Was she thinking about last night, about what had almost happened between them?

"Just…have a lot to do to wrap up loose ends. How much is the coffee? A couple of bucks?"

She reached into her purse but Max put his hand on hers.

"I'll take care of it."

She blinked, and looked like she wanted to say something. But then she cleared her throat as if changing her mind.

"Thanks, Max. Take care." And then she was rushing down the aisle and out of the diner.

Max watched her until she was driving down the street, her bodyguard following a few car lengths behind. Then he pitched some bills onto the table and headed out to his truck.

Once inside, he made a call to his boss and told him about the name that Bex had remembered.

"Where are you right now?" the chief asked.

"Eva-Marie's. Just had breakfast."

"Good. That's a hop-skip away from the Piggly Wiggly. This Reggie thing sounds like a great lead. And this is the perfect time to follow up on it. I sent Colby, Donna and Blake to the Pig to walk the witnesses through the shooting, step-by-step, to see if any of their initial statements change. Plus, we asked the manager to round everyone up who works there to come in, not just the ones on shift during the shooting. I wanted to see whether anyone saw anything suspicious in the days or weeks before, when maybe the shooters were casing the place to plan the assault. Everyone should be there right now. You can head on over and see if one of them is named Reggie."

"Will do. Wait, you said Blake is there?"

"You got a problem with that? The man isn't exactly a rookie at law enforcement. He's just new to us. He needs to be brought up to speed on how we do things."

Max grinned but was careful not to laugh. "You're the boss."

"Don't you forget that. Now get over there. And let me know once you find this Reggie guy."

WHEN MAX REACHED the doors to the grocery store, he flashed his badge to the deputy assigned to log everyone who went in or out. Then he was inside, taking quick stock of the situation.

A row of folding tables and chairs had been set up in the main aisle that ran the width of the store, just behind the checkout area. He counted fifteen civilians, mostly teenagers, sitting at the tables. They pretty much all had the same bored look that teenagers often sported these days as they apparently waited to be interviewed.

Many of them he recognized, by sight if not by name. In a town as small as Destiny, it was common to run into the same people at local stores and events, even if they never spoke. But there were still a few faces he didn't know, and some he couldn't see because they were blocked by others.

A short distance away were two more tables, each with only one civilian sitting behind it. Donna sat at one table, writing something down while her interviewee spoke animatedly with his hands to punctuate whatever he was saying. At the second table, Colby was the one asking questions, with Blake taking notes like a good apprentice should.

Colby spotted Max and waved him over. "Hey, if you're here to help interview, we sure could use you. Drag one of those tables over here."

"Which one's Reggie?"

"Reggie?" Colby frowned and picked up a clipboard of names. "Reggie, Reggie, Reggie." He ran his finger down the line, then reversed direction. "Hmm, no Reggie here."

"You mean Gina," the man sitting across from him said. He pointed to one of the names on the sheet of paper. "Gina Oliver. We all call her Reggie."

"Why?" Colby asked.

He shrugged. "Her real name is Regina. To most people she's Gina. But to her friends, she's Reggie. Beats me why she uses that for a nickname. I like Regina a lot better."

"Which one is she?" Max asked.

The young man leaned back in his chair, scanning the faces of the other employees. "There she is, on the end."

"Red hair?" Max grabbed an extra clipboard and pen from the table.

"Nah, brown hair." He stood and pointed. "That's her, next to the redhead. The one in the green shirt."

The young woman he was pointing to looked at Max and her eyes widened—just like they had the morning of the shooting, when he'd pulled her to the floor, supposedly to protect her from the gunmen.

"Oh, she's definitely involved in this," he muttered. "She was the cashier in my line when the gunmen busted into the store."

He dropped the clipboard on the table and stalked toward her.

She jumped up from her chair and took off toward the entrance.

Max took off after her.

Some of the other workers whistled and made catcalls as Reggie shoved a display of potato chips over and raced past a cash register.

Max hurdled over the display, bags of chips crunching beneath his feet as he sprinted toward the door where she'd just disappeared. He ran through the opening and slid to a halt in front of the deputy stationed there.

"Which way?" Max demanded. "The girl who ran out of here. Which way did she go?"

He pointed to the right, and Max caught a glimpse of her brown hair before she disappeared around the corner of the building. Dang, she was fast. Remembering the layout of the store on the lot and what was behind it, he took a gamble and headed in the opposite direction.

"You're going the wrong way," the cop called behind him.

Max ignored him, pumping his arms and legs as he rounded the corner, then sprinted for the next corner. If he remembered right, the tall fence at the back of the property would force his prey back toward him. Sure enough, as soon as he reached the corner, Reggie ran out in front of him. He tackled her in midstride, turning with her in his arms to protect her as they both fell.

Her startled scream was abruptly cut off when they landed in a heap of arms and legs. Max cursed when his head slammed against the pavement, but he held on to the squirming girl.

"Stop fighting me," he ordered.

The fury in his voice must have shocked her into submission, because she immediately stilled.

The sound of running footsteps heralded the arrival of Colby, the stun gun in his hand his weapon of choice against the rowdy teenager in Max's arms. He stopped a few feet away and clipped the stun gun back on his belt.

"Looks like you got your man—or woman or child, as the case may be."

"Stop grinning and get her off me."

"Yes, sir," Colby teased. He yanked the girl up then put her on the ground again, facedown, while he cuffed her.

Max was slower to get up, brushing off his pants and then rubbing the back of his head. He winced when his fingers touched a particularly tender spot that was already becoming a knot.

"Hold still," Colby ordered as he patted down the now squirming girl, checking for weapons. He straightened, keeping one hand on Reggie's right arm. "You okay?"

"No," she whined. "He threw me down. I probably have bruises. I'm gonna sue both of you."

"I wasn't talking to you," Colby said. "I was talking to the police officer who had to chase your sorry butt."

She glared at him.

"I'm fine. Just a bump." Max lowered his hand. "Are you Gina Oliver? The one they call Reggie?"

"Depends on who's asking." If she'd been chewing gum she'd probably have spit it at him. "Why'd you chase me? I ain't done nothing."

"So it's just a coincidence that you were at the cash register when your friends came in firing automatic weapons, huh?"

She looked away. "Friends? Don't know what you're talking about. Like I said, I didn't do anything."

"Then why did you run?"

She shrugged. "You're a big guy. You scared me. I've seen TV. I know how you cops can be, beating people up for no reason."

Colby rolled his eyes. "I'll clear the break room. We can interview her in there."

Max grabbed her arm and led her around the side of the building, following Colby.

Reggie swore at him. "I'm just a minimum-wage cashier. I ain't broke any laws. I didn't do anything wrong."

"Then you've got nothing to worry about."

A few minutes later, Max had Reggie cooling her heels in the locked break room while he spoke to Colby and Donna in the hallway a few doors down, just outside the manager's office. Donna had run over to them when they brought Reggie back inside.

She was slightly out of breath from zipping across the width of the store to catch them. "Max, you'd better be careful, and fast with the questions. I just got the lowdown on Gina. She's Sam Oliver's daughter."

Max groaned. "The Olivers who live off Coonskin Hollow?"

"Yep."

Colby frowned. "I don't remember Sam Oliver. Should I?"

"He's caused some trouble here and there. Maybe you were on vacation and I was the lucky one those nights," Max said.

"It gets worse," Donna warned him. "Sam heard we brought Reggie in for another interview and is on his way over. Says to leave his girl alone and no one is to speak to her. Of course, legally, she's an adult."

"Which means I can ask her anything I want." Max checked his watch. "Lucky for me I took her phone when I patted her down again in there. And as long as no one else is allowed down this hallway, no one's going to tell her that Daddy dearest is on his way. When did he call?"

"Hasn't been that long," Donna said. "I figure if he drives the speed limit, you've got fifteen minutes."

"Meaning I probably have ten."

"That's my guess. Make it quick."

Chapter Eleven

As soon as Max stepped inside the break room, Reggie jumped out of her chair and rushed toward the door.

Max shut the door and stepped in front of her, blocking her way. "You try to leave without answering my questions and I'll slap you in jail."

"On what charges?" she demanded.

"Conspiracy to commit armed robbery, for one. I can think of at least half a dozen other charges. You don't believe me, try it."

She glared at him, then turned around in a huff and plopped down on the plastic chair.

He eyed one of the delicate-looking chairs, not confident at all that it would be able to hold him up. But he took his chances and carefully sat down. The chair squeaked in protest but seemed sturdier than it looked. He rested his forearms on the table.

"Which one of those five yokels the other day was your boyfriend?"

She shook her head. "None of them. I don't... I don't have a boyfriend."

"You're a pretty good actress. I bought your scared act and thought I was protecting you when the gunmen stormed the place. Let me guess. That whole screaming thing was to let your boyfriend know something had gone wrong with the plan. As soon as you saw me in line you were worried, because a cop being there didn't figure into the whole plan, did it?"

She wouldn't look him in the eye. "I don't know what you're talking about. Some guys with guns came in the store and one of them shot at me. If it weren't for you, I'd probably be dead. Not that I'm thanking you or anything."

"Yeah. I'm not holding my breath for a kumbaya moment with you, either."

"I don't even know what that means."

"That doesn't surprise me, either. Try going to church sometime. Learn a few hymns. Learn not to hang with gangbangers hell-bent on spending the rest of their lives in prison and dragging you with them."

She blinked, a shadow of fear flashing in her eyes before she looked away. Crossing her arms, she seemed to be trying for a jaded, world-weary look. If he hadn't seen her eyes, he'd probably have bought her routine. He wasn't kidding when he'd said she was a good actress. And he supposed there was a remote possibility that she really was telling the truth. But he wasn't counting on it. Not since Bex had told him one of the gunmen had mentioned a Reggie. He figured he'd lead with that and see where the conversation went from there.

"See, here's the thing, Reggie. I don't believe you. Wanna know why? Because one of the customers hiding in the store during the shooting overheard a couple of those gunmen talking about the whole thing. You know, the plan to go after Bex Kane? The plan where you called them when she came into the store. And later, you called them saying she was heading toward the front. I thought you looked familiar when I saw you at the register and now I know why. You walked past the deli when Bex was there. I'm guessing that was your reconnaissance so you could estimate how much longer it would be before Bex would check out. So your buddies could time it with their entrance. What did you do, fake a price check or tell the manager you needed a bathroom break when Bex walked into the store? So you could keep an eye on her and warn your buddies when it looked like she was about done shopping?"

Her eyes were like saucers now and looked like

they were about to bug out of her head. He hadn't actually seen her near the deli. But based on what Bex had said, he figured she must have hidden close by, maybe one aisle over, peeking through the shelves to watch Bex. It only made sense. And from the borderline terrified expression on the girl's face now, he knew he'd guessed right.

He glanced at his watch. He didn't have much time before Reggie's father arrived. No question the man would put an end to the interview and insist on a lawyer if the cops wanted to talk to her again. Her dad was an ex-con and had no love for the police. He also knew the system, and his rights. And his daughter's.

He was lucky Reggie had even come back to the store with the other employees for an interview. The manager must have called her when her father wasn't home, or he'd never have let her come in. Max decided it was time to play hardball, to turn the screws and try to get as much info as possible before he lost his chance.

"The way I see it, Reggie, you have two options. One, I haul you off to jail and arrest you on attempted-murder charges."

"But I didn't do anything. I was with you. And then the manager put me in the cooler with the others. I had no part in this."

"I already told you I have a witness, so you can drop the act. There's no question that you knew about the assault ahead of time, helped plan it and now you're trying to cover it up. That's conspiracy to commit murder. Makes you just as guilty as if you'd worn one of those masks and pulled the trigger. You can forget college or whatever else you might have planned. You're going to spend your twenties inside a maximum-security prison."

She swallowed, hard. "What's the second option?"

He had her. If he could just get her to give him the info before Daddy dearest showed up.

"You give me their names, for starters. Oh, we know most of them. Some of them are turning deals in the hospital and lockup," he lied. He wasn't counting Lenny, since he didn't know enough to help with the case. "Then you have to tell me exactly why they were trying to kill Bex Kane."

"If...if I do that, do I still go to jail?"

"Prison, Reggie. Yeah, you're doing time no matter what. But I could put a good word in with the judge and try to get you in a minimum-security facility for a reduced sentence." He shrugged. "If you fully cooperate, who knows? Maybe you'll even get off with only probation."

He was lying through his teeth. But she didn't know that. A commotion sounded from out in the main part of the grocery store. It sounded like

Colby arguing with someone—probably Reggie's father. Max was almost out of time.

"Tell me right now, Reggie. Names. Or I take you to jail."

She spewed the names out like a rapid spitting a kayak down a rain-swollen river.

He scribbled them down as the sound of yelling and shoes pounding on the floor outside got louder and louder.

"They weren't trying to kill her, either," she volunteered. "Did the ones turning deals tell you that already?"

She was so ready to sing, worried someone else would get a better deal than her. If he only had more time.

"Maybe, maybe not. Just hurry and tell me what you know before I decide not to talk to the judge on your behalf."

"They were supposed to scare her, for one thing. And then they were gonna take her—"

More yelling sounded down the hallway, much closer now.

Reggie's eyes widened, and she looked toward the door.

Max slammed his hands down on the table, making her jump.

"Finish it, Reggie. They were going to kidnap Miss Kane? Is that what you're saying?"

"Yes. For a little while, at least. They definitely weren't wanting to kill anyone."

"You seriously expect me to believe that? They had assault rifles. They were searching for her. Of course they wanted to hurt her."

"They didn't. I swear. They were supposed to—"

"Reggie, shut your face!" A shout sounded from right outside the room. "Don't tell them cops nothing."

Her eyes widened again, and she chewed her bottom lip in indecision.

The sound of scuffles sounded from outside. Something heavy slammed against the wall. It sounded like half of the police force was trying to keep her father from coming into the room.

She obviously wasn't sure what to do. She kept glancing from the door to Max.

"Reggie, ask for a lawyer, you idiot!" her father raged outside.

She slid a look at Max, her earlier smug look returning.

"Think very carefully before you say anything else," Max warned her. "Remember, you need me to give a good word to the judge to help you get a reduced sentence. And I'll only do that if you tell me what those boys wanted when they broke into the store. What were they going to do? Why were they looking for Bex? Who hired them? Give me something, Reggie."

She looked toward the door again, where they could both hear her father yelling.

Max straightened. "Fine. You want to spend your twenties and thirties in prison, that's your choice." He turned around and strode toward the door.

"Wait!"

He turned around. "Yes?"

"They were supposed to take her someplace else. I don't know where, I swear. But they were supposed to make her talk, on camera."

"Talk about what?"

"They wanted her to confess to murdering some guy named Bobby something or other."

He grew very still. "Caldwell? Bobby Caldwell?"

"That's it. Yes. They were supposed to film her making a confession. And then they were supposed to give the film to—"

The door slammed open, the frame splintering in pieces where the locking mechanism used to be. Six-foot-six, three-hundred-pound Sam Oliver stood in the opening, looking like a bull ready to tear into a matador. He glared at Max then turned his glare on his daughter. He jabbed his finger in the air, pointing at her. "Don't tell him another damn thing."

She nodded, looking more terrified of her

father than of Max, which, of course, meant his interview had just come to an end. If he'd had any doubts, they went away the second she finally found her voice again.

"I want a lawyer."

Chapter Twelve

She'd forgotten how bright and clear the night sky could be out in the country, the stars sparkling like little gems without the light pollution of a city to compete with them. Bex absently traced a finger on the arm of the white wicker couch in the little sunroom on the back of her mother's house. Only, it could be more aptly called a moon room right now, since it was past ten at night. She'd always loved this room, which her daddy had converted from a screened-in porch when she was in elementary school. He was handy like that, always doing projects around the house to make her mama happy.

"Are you okay, Bex?"

She let out a squeal of surprise and jerked around to see Max standing in the doorway between the kitchen and the sunroom. She pressed her hand to her chest, surprised her heart hadn't exploded from fright.

"Max? What on earth are you doing here? How did you even get in?"

"Sorry," he said. "Didn't mean to frighten you. I drove by, saw your lights on and decided to stop. I knocked, loudly, several times. But you must not have heard me all the way back here. When you didn't answer, I got worried so I used my key."

He held it up, then pitched it onto one of the little wicker tables scattered around the room.

"Your mom gave me that key years ago. I used to keep an eye on the place whenever she went on a trip out of town. She liked me to come inside, water her plants. But mainly she wanted me to make sure the pipes hadn't burst or anything else major happened." He cocked his head, studying Bex. "She never told me outright that she was visiting you in Knoxville. But it wasn't hard to figure out. Word gets around town when a limo shows up with out of town plates."

He stepped closer, rounding the couch. Then he stopped abruptly. Even with the room lit only by moonlight she could tell he was looking at her, his eyes glittering as they traveled down her barely clothed body.

Her face flamed hot and she grabbed an afghan off the back of the couch to cover herself. She was only wearing a nightshirt and panties. True, Max had seen her in far less. But that was a lifetime ago.

He sighed and pulled a folder out from under his arm and plopped it onto the narrow table in front of the couch. "We need to talk."

She waved toward the folder. "About whatever's in there?"

"That and more. I don't suppose I can tempt you into a late-night trip to the police station for an on-camera interview."

"Are you ever going to stop asking me that?"

"Not as long as my boss keeps bugging me to ask you."

She rolled her eyes again. "The only way I'll go there is if rocky road ice cream is involved. With fresh strawberries on top."

The corner of his mouth quirked up. "And chocolate syrup?"

"You remember."

"I remember a lot of things."

She tightened her grip on the afghan.

He gave her a sad smile this time. "This town still rolls up the streets at nine. The ice-cream parlor closed hours ago. Unless you want to grab something from Smiths? Not that a twenty-four-hour convenience store compares well to an ice-cream parlor."

If they kept skirting around memories of their shared past, she was doomed. She didn't respond to his ice-cream comments and tried to bring the conversation back to something less dangerous.

"You said you drove by and saw my lights on. I may not have been to your new house, but you said it's on land that borders your dad's property. My mom's house isn't anywhere near that."

"I didn't say I happened to be in the neighborhood. I was hoping you'd be up. Like I said, we need to talk."

"Okay, well, I guess I'll try to answer your questions. I just can't go back to the police station, okay? I'm serious. You have no idea how awful it was. Your boss locked me up in one of those cells for two days. I was eighteen and terrified. The only reason he let me out was because he didn't have enough evidence to charge me and the judge ordered me released."

"I know. I was there, remember?" His jaw worked. "Or I would have been, if you'd let me. I had to hear everything secondhand because you refused to let me visit you. The chief would have allowed that if you'd only told him to let me in."

"What did you expect me to do? You'd asked me to marry you and I turned you down. Then a few hours later I was in jail under suspicion of murder. I was confused, scared and angry. I couldn't deal with your hurt feelings on top of everything else."

His eyes flashed with anger. "My *hurt feelings*? You make it sound so trite. It was a hell of a lot more than hurt feelings. Why did you shut me out? Why didn't you…"

He closed his eyes, shaking his head. When he looked at her again, the anger seemed to have drained out of him. "This is a conversation we should have had a decade ago. It's too late to go over all that now." He flipped the folder open. "This is the reason I'm here." He spread out some pictures on the table, then frowned. "Mind if I turn on a light? The kitchen light isn't doing a lot of good out here."

She adjusted the afghan and cleared her throat. "Go ahead." She didn't bother to tell him where the switch was. He knew this house just as well as she did.

He crossed to the side wall, well away from any doorways, and leaned down by the baseboard to flip the switch. Light flooded the room from the ceiling fan overhead. He sat on the wicker chair across from her. "Your father had a thing for putting the switches in the craziest places, didn't he?"

"He called it his security system. Anyone breaking in wouldn't know how to turn on any lights."

"That's for sure. I bet it makes for some stubbed toes at night, though."

She shook her head. "I'm used to it. Except for

all the boxes in the living room, of course. I'm still banging my shins against those, day or night."

His smile faded at the reminder that she was packing up the house to leave. He fanned the pictures out again.

She scooted forward, careful to keep the afghan tucked around her. "Those look like hospital photos. Five guys. The gunmen again?"

"Yeah. Better pics than the ones on my phone. Are you sure that you don't recognize any of them?"

"Do you know their names yet?" She picked up the first picture.

"We do now, yes. From a witness at the grocery store. Plus, Blake, one of the new detectives, worked with some of his contacts at his old job to corroborate the information. We'd have figured out their names anyway from their prints since they're all in the system. But that was taking a while. Regardless, I'm more interested right now in finding out whether you've seen them around, maybe watching you in the days leading up to the assault."

"Watching me? Like…stalking me?"

He nodded.

A shiver went down her spine and she set the first picture down, then carefully studied each of the remaining ones before shaking her head.

"Sorry, Max. I don't think I've seen any of these men before. Or, boys, really. How old are they?"

"They range in age from nineteen to twenty-two. But don't feel sorry for them. They're old enough to make better decisions. And this isn't their first brush with the law. They all belong to the same gang."

She gave him a sharp look. "We have gangs in Destiny now?"

He laughed without humor. "Even a town this small has its own version of gangs. But, no, they're not from here. That's why I want to make absolutely sure that you look carefully at their faces. Think back over the last few weeks, even."

After looking over the pictures again, she pitched them onto the table. "I haven't seen any of them before. They must be from Knoxville, since you're making such a big deal over whether I've seen them before."

He shuffled the pictures into the folder and leaned back against the chair. "Can't confirm or deny that."

"You don't have to. I can still read you, just like I always could." As soon as she said it, she wished she could take the words back. "I'm sorry. I'm not trying to rehash the past. Really, I'm not. It just seems like every conversation we have takes us there, sooner or later."

"Don't apologize. Sitting with you here is…

weird, strange. Not what I expected I'd be doing this week, that's for sure."

She smiled. "Me neither."

He checked his watch, then swore beneath his breath.

"My mama would have washed your mouth out with soap for that back in the day."

He grinned. "You're right. She would have. Guess I've picked up some bad habits I need to work on. I'll get to the point, since it's getting late. We've made a lot of progress on the investigation."

"Which one?"

He stilled. "Sorry, I forgot to tell you about Marcia with everything else that's been going on. She confessed to shooting the rifle but swears it was only to scare you. She said it wasn't planned, that she had her gun in her car and after seeing you here with me she got to thinking about Bobby—whom she fancied her boyfriend, even though from what I remember he was always telling her to get lost—and as she was driving away she pulled over and decided to try to scare you just to make herself feel better, I guess. She thinks you killed him."

She rubbed her hands up and down her arms. "Her and about half the town."

He didn't bother to deny the obvious. Half

the town, or more, did think she'd killed Bobby Caldwell. She shivered again.

"Are you cold?" He started to shrug out of his jacket.

"No, no. I'm fine. Thanks. So you let Marcia go, right?"

"Hell, no. I want you to press charges against her for attempted murder."

"But she wasn't trying to kill me."

He gave her an incredulous look. "She shot a rifle at you."

She shook her head. "If she was trying to kill me, I'd be dead, wouldn't I? Marcia was an amazing shot even back in high school. If she says she was just trying to scare me, I believe her."

He shook his head. "You're saying you don't want to press charges."

"That's what I'm saying."

He shook his head again. "Unbelievable. Fine, I'll tell the chief. Back to the grocery store investigation. I've got some questions for you. But first let me explain a few things. I probably shouldn't be telling you any of this. Well, no probably about it. The investigation is confidential, and I need your word that you won't share these details with anyone else."

"It's not like I'm receiving social invitations in this town. Who would I tell?"

"I'm serious. Your lawyer, a clerk at the bank, anyone at all. Not a word."

"Okay, okay. I won't tell anyone."

"When you and I talked at the diner, you told me that one of the gunmen said Reggie told them a woman was heading toward the checkout. That set off alarm bells for me. It sounded like the gunmen had inside information, someone inside the store, maybe an employee, letting them know when it was the right time to come inside."

"The right time? Like when there weren't that many customers?"

"More like when *you* were inside."

"Me? You really were serious earlier when you said I might have been the target?"

He slowly nodded.

She listened in stunned disbelief as he told her about a cashier named Reggie who'd partnered with the gunmen. Her hand shook as she pulled the afghan closer. "You're saying that someone is trying to…kidnap me? They want to force me to…confess?"

"According to Reggie, yes."

"Well. I guess we know who's behind that. It's Mr. Caldwell, Bobby's father. Has to be."

He nodded. "Makes sense. That's the first person I thought of, too. He's got plenty of money, owns thousands of acres of farmland in this county, and his family comes from old money up in Chattanooga. Plus, he's made no secret over the years that he always thought you did it. After all, you and Bobbie had a...history."

She frowned and was about to dress him down when he held up a hand to stop her.

"I'm not blaming the victim here. I know he stalked you during your senior year. *History* was the wrong word."

"You think? Yet another reason I'm no fan of your boss, by the way. He didn't do anything to stop Bobby. No one did."

He winced.

She immediately regretted her outburst. "Except you. I know you tried to help me, got yourself in trouble more times than I can count by going after him."

"Fat lot of good it did. His father's security guys tossed me on my butt just about every time before I could get close to Bobby. I'm really sorry, Bex. I'm sorry I didn't do more. I know it was a really tough time for you."

"Tough?" She fisted her hands in the afghan. "No one could help me—not the school, not my mom, not you, not the police. I was miserable, Max. My life was a living hell that year." She sucked in a breath and looked at him, too late wishing she could recall her words. "I don't mean that you and I—I mean, it was also the best year."

"After Bobby was found," he continued, as

if she'd never spoken, "his father kept lobbying Thornton to arrest you. But, like you said, there was never enough evidence. So after that initial forty-eight hours in the cell, he had to let you go."

"Yeah, nice guy. Holding a terrified teenager in jail after ignoring her calls for help for nearly a year."

"Bex, that was a long time ago. Looking back, can't you see there was more to it than that? He was also protecting you. From Bobby's father. Those two days were a cooling-off period for everyone. Thornton feels terrible about failing you, not being able to do anything about the stalking without proof. He was determined to protect you from the fallout."

"Let me guess," she said. "He told you that? Because he sure hasn't ever said anything like that to me."

"Not exactly. But I was there, too, spoke to him more than you in those early days, since you wouldn't let me visit you. I figured out what he was doing even if he was too gruff and stubborn to explain his actions." He shook his head. "He's never been one to explain himself. But I've worked with him since I graduated. Aside from odd jobs on farms and mowing yards, being a cop in Destiny is the only real job I've ever had. So I've had plenty of time to get to know him. He's a good man, Bex. Locking you up wasn't out of meanness or because he really thought you'd killed Bobby. Believe it or not, he cared what happened to you."

She stared past him, through the windows to the dark backyard, illuminated only by moonlight. Max might be able to see some good in Thornton. But she'd never experienced anything but the harsh reality of a policeman who did things by the book and wouldn't help her no matter how many times she pleaded for him to stop the stalking. And then the moment something happened to Bobby, he'd locked her up. She'd never forgive him for that.

"You think Robert Caldwell Senior hired those men to go after me?" she asked, refusing to discuss Thornton anymore.

He let out a deep sigh. "I think it's possible, highly likely. But while some of the other guys track down that lead and talk to Mr. Caldwell, I'm here to talk to you. Bex—"

"You want me to tell you about that night."

He nodded. "Your mother, God rest her soul, thought she was protecting you by not letting you talk to the police back then. But the problem is that it only makes you look guilty. Bobby's father has built this up in his mind for years, convinced that because you left town, you must have been guilty."

"I didn't leave until two weeks later. It's not like I just disappeared overnight."

"Doesn't make much difference. You never gave a statement. The investigation stagnated because of it. In Caldwell's eyes, you're guilty. Period. And he's gone ten years without someone paying for his son's death. You show up in town, he hears about it and bam, gunmen raid the store when you're there and go searching for you, paid by some anonymous guy."

"Anonymous?"

He nodded. "One of the gunmen in the hospital wanted to cut a deal. But the deal was to give us the identity of whoever hired him and the others to go after you. He couldn't give us his identity."

"How much money are we talking?"

"Ten thousand dollars. Each."

"Wow. Fifty thousand dollars is more than the average person could afford. But ten thousand apiece wasn't exactly making those guys rich. I wouldn't risk my freedom for a penny less than a million," she joked.

"I didn't say they were smart."

She smiled. "What exactly do you need from me? Do you want me to say I didn't do it? That I didn't kill Bobby?"

"That would be a good place to start."

The silence stretched out between them.

"Bex—"

"You need to leave."

His brows raised. "Back up. What just happened here?"

"Nothing happened. It's late and I'm exhausted. I need to get some sleep. So do you." Holding the afghan around her like a robe, she stood and headed into the kitchen.

Max followed her. She could hear him close and lock the door to the sunroom behind him. By the time he caught up to her, she had the front door standing wide-open.

His gaze flicked to the door, then to her. "What time do you get up in the morning? I'll bring breakfast and then we can continue with our conversation."

She shook her head. "I'm not answering any more questions. Don't bother stopping by."

His brows lowered in a deep slash. "I'm trying to help you, Bex."

"No. You're trying to solve a case and you think that by dredging up the past you'll find some clue. Well, you can do that all you want, but you'll have to do it without me."

He stepped closer, looking down at her with a deep frown wrinkling his brow. "I could arrest you for obstructing a police investigation."

"Go ahead. Then you and Thornton can share some stories over a couple of beers about how you both threw me in jail."

His eyes narrowed, but not before she saw the flash of hurt in them.

Her shoulders slumped. "I'm sorry, Max. I shouldn't have said—"

He stepped through the door without another word.

Chapter Thirteen

Bex towel-dried the breakfast dishes and packed them into a box. That was the last of them. From here on out, however many days she had left in Destiny, she'd use paper plates and disposable utensils. Tomorrow was trash day. She'd empty the refrigerator tonight and set the bags at the curb.

She'd already had her RAV4 taken to Eddie's to get the windshield fixed. Ralph, the owner, was going to sell her mom's Taurus for her. Movers were scheduled to arrive later in the week to take the boxes she'd designated to go to her condo in Knoxville. Then, as soon as her lawyer gave the okay, an auction company would hold an estate sale for everything else, including the house. In just a few short weeks, it would be as if her mother had never even existed.

A sob escaped before Bex even registered the

tears flowing down her cheeks. Her knees buckled and she sagged to the floor.

"Oh, Mama. Mama, Mama, Mama. I miss you so much."

The grief hit her like a tidal wave, pushing her under, drowning her in darkness and sorrow. She'd cried when she'd first gotten the call from the hospital, of course. But that was nothing compared to the paralyzing pain that racked her now. She curled into a ball and cried until it seemed like there was no moisture left in her body to form any tears, until her throat ached from the strength of her sobs. And then she fell into an exhausted slumber right there on the kitchen floor.

When she woke up, only a short time had passed. But it felt like a lifetime. Her lifetime, her mother's, her family's. Nothing would ever be the same again. She'd never hear her mother's voice on the phone. Never see her smiling face when the limo pulled up to Bex's condo for one of her mom's trips to Knoxville. Never swap much-loved books in the mail with favorite passages highlighted in pink. Bex had thought she'd dealt with her grief before coming back to Destiny. But apparently she'd had to see the house all packed up to really push her over the edge and make her face her tremendous loss.

Feeling bruised from the emotional hit she'd just taken, she pushed herself up to sitting and rubbed her bleary eyes. This little house had been her home for eighteen years. She'd been happy here, the doted upon only child of two incredibly loving parents. Now both of them were gone. And Bex wasn't sure how she could go on without them.

She was tempted to curl back into a ball. But she could almost see her mother scowling at her and telling her to "suck it up, Buttercup." Her mom never suffered whining or pity parties. Bex wasn't going to insult her memory now by ignoring all the life lessons her mama had taught her.

After replenishing her parched body with a bottle of water, Bex went outside to check the mail that she'd forgotten to check yesterday. That was one more thing she needed to do, set up a forwarding address. She supposed she could do that online tonight.

The bodyguard assigned to watch her this morning sat in his SUV parked in the grass across the street, no longer bothering to pretend that she didn't know about them.

She waved and he waved back. Having him there made her feel safe. But she cringed at the thought of how much the twenty-four-hour security was costing Max. As soon as she sold her mom's house she'd pay him back. She'd caused enough problems for him. Having him lose his savings wasn't going to be added to that list.

She opened the mailbox and pulled out the short stack of envelopes—a final bill from the funeral home, the electric bill and a manila envelope with no return address or stamp. She hesitated, a cold prickle of unease flashing through her.

It wasn't uncommon for people this far from town to stick a note in each other's mailboxes. It was most likely a note from one of her mother's friends, wishing her condolences. But with everything that had happened since her fateful trip to the Piggly Wiggly, the envelope took on a more sinister appearance.

The sound of shoes crunching on dried leaves had her looking up to see the bodyguard crossing the road toward her. He stopped in front of her.

"Miss Kane, I'm Neil Granger. I couldn't help noticing the worry on your face. Something wrong?"

"Maybe. It seems silly, really, but this—"

"Didn't go through the post office." He frowned down at the envelope. "Mind if I open it?"

Since he was already pulling on a pair of latex gloves, she didn't bother answering. When he was ready, she handed it to him.

"Please step back," he said.

Her throat tightened at his request. Did he think someone had hidden something dangerous inside? It didn't seem possible, as thin as the envelope was. But she stepped back anyway, watching him carefully pat down the surface and examine the edges before pulling the flap open. He peeked inside, then his posture seemed to relax and he motioned her forward.

"It's some kind of picture." He reached in and pulled it out. His gaze shot to hers, and he slowly turned the picture around.

Bex blinked in shock as the proof of her sins stared up at her from an eight-by-ten glossy photo. She couldn't fool herself any longer. This wasn't something she could run away from again. It was time to finally face her past.

MAX PROPPED HIS booted feet on top of his desk and leaned back in his chair, watching the sun burn away the last of the morning fog through the police station windows. Yet another chilly day had dawned with no viable leads about who had arranged for the gangbangers to go after Bex in the grocery store. To say that he was getting frustrated was an understatement.

One desk over from him in the expansive squad room, Colby was leaning back in his chair, too. Both of them had the case files up on their computer monitors and were tossing theories back and forth.

"The Marcia thing is still bothering me," Colby said.

"Tell me about it. I didn't expect her to be released so quickly. She should be toughing it out in a jail cell right now."

Colby jabbed a thumb over his shoulder at the chief, who was talking to Donna by the interrogation room. "His orders. When you didn't call back saying Miss Kane wanted to press charges, he wouldn't let us lock her up. Sorry, man."

"Nothing you could do. I'd just feel better if she wasn't on the loose with that rifle. If she told us the truth, then her emotions are running high and impairing her judgment. What's to stop her from deciding to go after Bex again?"

"And if she's lying?"

"Then maybe whoever hired the gang to hold up the grocery store hired her, too. What did we find on Caldwell senior? Do we have anything at all to link him to any of this? His belief that Bex killed his son is no secret. And he certainly has the funds to hire anyone he wants to do just about anything."

Colby dipped his head in acknowledgment. "Donna's been following that angle and so far she's got nothing. Obviously he's too sick right now to have gone to Knoxville. And we can't get a look at his finances to look for payments to any thugs without a warrant. Trust me. Donna tried. But the judge turned her down, said he needs something more than conjecture."

"Did she interview him?"

"Officially, no. He's refusing to talk to us. But she caught up to him outside the hospital before one of his chemo treatments. She barraged him with questions as his son, Deacon, pushed his father into the hospital. Didn't do any good and his lawyer called the chief later threatening a lawsuit for harassment if we pulled something like that again."

Max shook his head. "Other than what I got from Lenny Stinsky, we've got nothing from the shooters, either. None of them are talking. I'll give it to Caldwell senior, or whoever is behind this, they picked the right thugs to hire. Or maybe threatened them with some dire consequence if they talked."

He tapped his right hand on his thigh, thinking it through. "Lenny and the other one who was shot are still in the hospital. Maybe we can play them against each other, even with their lawyers present, and get one of them to take a deal."

"I thought Lenny Stinsky didn't know the name of the guy who hired them. That only leaves the Chucky guy. And he's a hard-core criminal. I don't see us getting him to go for a deal."

"He's facing hard time for the grocery store holdup."

Colby shrugged. "You can try to talk to him. I certainly didn't have any luck."

"Maybe I'll head over there in a little bit." Max tapped his thigh again. "Even if he doesn't have a name, he's got to have a better description, maybe even of the make and model of the car. If we can narrow it down, get the specific date when it happened, too, we might generate a viable lead on who was in that car that night."

"Like I said, I already tried. But hey, maybe after stewing in the hospital for a few days he's softened up. Or getting worried about heading to jail when he gets discharged. Caldwell seems like the logical money man. Maybe one of his security guys is the man who drove to Knoxville. I can work up a list of everyone who works for him and—"

"Already did."

They both turned to see Donna standing a few feet away. The chief was still on the far side of the room, talking to Blake this time.

"Did what?" Colby asked.

"Got a list of everyone working for Caldwell. I've even spoken to a few of them. But they all, of course, insist they haven't been to Knoxville. And ever since I tried to talk to their boss at the hospital, I'm persona non grata at the Caldwell estate. I haven't given up. But I'm spending most of my time on the computer looking into everyone instead of interviewing them. Slow going."

"Let's assume Caldwell is the money guy and

one of his security guys hired the thugs," Colby said. "Why now? If his goal was to get Bex to confess to murdering his son, why wait ten years to go after her?"

"Cancer," Max answered. "He's going through chemo. And he sure didn't look well when I saw him at his lawyer's office. Maybe he decided he's got nothing to lose by breaking the law and going after Bex. Maybe getting her to confess to murdering his son and going to prison is his last dying wish. Who else has a motive to want her to confess?"

"Marcia Knolls," Donna and Colby both said at the same time.

Max slowly nodded. "She's got motive. She loved Bobby and has always blamed Bex for his death. But the same question goes for her. Why wait ten years?"

Donna frowned and looked deep in thought.

Colby shrugged. "Beats me. Unless seeing Bex in town was enough to make Marcia go ballistic, like she did when she shot that rifle. Her family has a big farm outside of town. They aren't exactly hurting financially. Maybe she's got a piece of that pie and decided to use it to hire those wackos to scare Bex into confessing."

"Okay," Max said. "Robert Caldwell Senior and Marcia Knolls are still suspects. And we still have nothing concrete to charge either one."

Colby and Donna exchanged a frustrated look.

"There's something else bothering me about this whole thing," Max continued. "If the goal is to get Bex to confess, why make such a public thing out of it? Those thugs could have kidnapped Bex at her mom's house at any time since she got here. She doesn't have any neighbors close by. It would have been easy. So why wait until she's in the grocery store to go after her? Either of you have a theory on that?"

"Not me," Donna said. "And the chief's waving me over again. Probably to fuss at me for pushing so hard on the Caldwells again." She rolled her eyes and headed toward the other side of the room.

"I don't have a theory either," Colby said.

"I might," Max said. "But it's a bit out there. I was hoping you had something better."

"Well, I don't so you might as well share. Who knows? Maybe you're onto something. Spill."

Blake, who'd just sat down at his desk two rows over, must have heard their conversation, because he suddenly rolled his chair over in front of Colby's desk and crossed his arms, daring either of them to tell him to go away.

Colby frowned, obviously unimpressed with Blake's challenging posture. "Don't you have something to do? Like issue parking tickets down Main Street?"

"Leave him alone," Max said.

Colby's mouth twitched, and Max knew he was trying to hold back a smile. Picking on the new guy was more of a habit than anything else at this point. But Blake was a serious kind of guy and was getting more and more wound up. For both Blake's and Colby's sakes, it was time to move on and let the new guy start contributing.

"What's your theory?" Colby asked.

The relief on Blake's face was palpable. He sat at attention in his chair, eagerly waiting to hear what Max had to say.

"Okay, the Pig isn't far from the station, so as soon as a nine-one-one call went out, it was only a matter of minutes before some uniformed cops would show up, a few minutes more for the SWAT team since they had to gear up. And it's right in the middle of the main business area where most of our restaurants and shops are."

"Right," Colby said. "Which doesn't make sense, as you already said."

"It doesn't make sense if your goal is to get Bex to confess. But what if that isn't the goal?"

Colby frowned. "We already know that was the goal. That's the only useful information Lenny gave us."

"No. Lenny said the goal was to scare Bex. Reggie's the one who said they were going to kidnap her to tape a confession. We don't have corroboration on that yet. But Lenny isn't exactly a genius. He didn't ask questions and didn't really care why he did what he did. He was in it for the money, doing whatever Chucky told him to do. Maybe he thought the goal was to scare Bex. But he wasn't told the real reason for the Piggly Wiggly assault."

Colby nodded. "Okay. I'm with you. But you're thinking the real reason wasn't to kidnap Bex either?"

"Look at who was hired for the job. Budding criminals, gang members who want to prove to other gang members that they're tough, who think they're way more badass than they really are. Too stupid to think through the odds and realize they probably wouldn't make it out of that store without being caught. They saw easy money, something fun and illegal to add to their résumés to make them look even cooler to the rest of the gang. Heck, maybe the three without gang tats were doing it to earn full gang membership."

"Yeah. So?"

"Then you've got Lenny. Younger than the rest, a new gang member. Not hardened yet. He's a weak link, a really weak link. As soon as we started questioning him and threatening him with the usual cop lies, he started singing, told us everything he knew—which wasn't much, but the end result could very well be exactly what whoever planned this whole thing wanted."

Blake leaned forward, resting his arms on the edge of Colby's desk. "The guy behind it wanted the gunmen to be caught?"

Colby frowned at him, then looked at Max. "Is that your theory?"

"Yes, but follow it through to its logical conclusion. The guy behind this wanted the whole incident to be public so everyone in town would hear about it. And he was counting on Lenny to squeal. His goal wasn't to capture Miss Kane. His goal was to force the police to look into the Bobby Caldwell case again."

Colby blinked in surprise. "Makes sense in a weird kind of way. We always investigate the victim's past to see if there's a connection. That means looking at the old Caldwell case, too. You may be right. Pretty brilliant, in a sick kind of way. Which points the finger right back at Bobby Caldwell's father again. Robert Caldwell is bitter enough and rich enough to pull it off. And we already said he has nothing left to lose since he's terminally ill."

"What about the brother?" Blake asked.

"Deacon," Max said. "You think he might be behind this?"

"I think we should look into him, too, before jumping to any conclusions."

Colby narrowed his eyes. "Now look here, I'm not jumping to—"

"Stop," Max ordered. "You're both right. We need to focus on looking for a tangible link between any of the Caldwells and the gunmen. They had M16s. Those are military-issue. Deacon is ex-military. Maybe he's in on this and managed to get his hands on those guns. Has anyone traced the serial numbers yet?"

"Randy did that the first day," Colby said. "They're part of a shipment that was labeled as destroyed because they failed inspection. We're still following that angle to see how they ended up in those gangbangers' hands instead of being melted down for parts. Caldwell senior is ex-military, too, and a gun collector. Wouldn't surprise me if he's got some contacts who helped him get his hands on those rifles— assuming he's involved."

"It's all speculation for now but we need to follow the trail," Max said. "We're still right back to where we were. But having talked it all through, I feel like we're on the right track. We just have to hit them hard, help Donna dig up any information we can to piece together what the Caldwells and their hired hands were doing since Bex came to town. We need timelines, dates, places, witnesses. Let's get some pictures together of everyone who works for the Caldwells and circulate those around, see if anyone can help us build those timelines. We can show those pictures to some of the rental car companies in Knoxville to see whether they recognize any of them, since I highly doubt the Caldwells or their men would use their own car when they hired those gang-bangers. It's highly likely they rented one."

"That's good," Colby said. "I can follow up on the alibis and rental angles."

"I can help," Blake offered. "I can get the car companies in Knoxville to give us information without making us try to get a warrant, which we probably can't get right now."

"You're right," Colby agreed. "We probably couldn't get a warrant. Do it. That sounds good."

Blake jumped up and rolled his chair back to his desk. The sound of the keyboard clicking quickly followed.

"What about Marcia Knolls?" Colby said. "Are we not looking at her anymore?"

"I think we shouldn't rule anyone out yet. We'll work on a timeline for her as well, track her movements since Bex got into town. Who knows, maybe someone will remember seeing her talking to one of the Caldwells or their hired hands."

Colby stood and grabbed his jacket from the back of his chair.

"Where are you going?" Max asked.

"To the hospital. I'm going to see if I can't put

the screws on Chucky and Lenny and get a make and model on that car."

"Sounds good." Max stood. "I'll go with you. We can play good cop, bad cop."

"Only if I get to be the bad cop this time," Colby teased.

"We'll toss a coin."

Colby laughed and they both rounded their desks.

Max stopped, staring at the double glass front doors of the squad room. One of the bodyguards he'd hired was opening the door. And behind him was Bex.

BEX'S DARK HAIR swirled around her. She clutched her jacket closed against the light wind that was a precursor to the storm that Mable Humphries had predicted days ago.

Beside Max, Colby said, "Wow. Never thought I'd see her voluntarily come here. You think maybe something else happened?"

That was exactly what Max was worried about. Bex's face was paler than he'd ever seen it. And he couldn't think of a single reason for her bodyguard to have brought her here unless something terrible had happened.

As soon as she saw Max, a look of relief seemed to pass over Bex's face and she hurried toward him.

"Max, thank goodness. Are you okay?" she asked, her eyes searching his.

Max frowned in confusion at the bodyguard standing next to her before looking at her again. "I'm fine. What happened? Did someone try to shoot you again?"

Her eyes widened. "No. No, nothing like that." She half turned and motioned toward the man beside her. "Mr. Granger, the picture please."

"What picture?" Max asked.

In answer, the bodyguard held up a manila envelope. Max noted he was wearing a latex glove, so he automatically grabbed one for himself out of the top drawer of the closest desk and yanked it on before taking the envelope.

The frightened look on Bex's face, and the way she kept glancing at the chief on the other side of the room still talking to Donna, told Max something was very wrong. The little hairs were standing up on the back of his neck. And he didn't like the determined glint in Bex's eyes, like she'd made some kind of important decision. Whatever had brought her here, he wished she'd spoken to him in private about it first.

"That was in my mailbox this morning," she explained. "The mail comes in the afternoon. But I forgot to check it yesterday. As soon as I saw what was inside, I had Mr. Granger drive me straight here."

Max pulled out the picture, then stared at it in surprise. Whatever he'd expected, it wasn't this—an eight by ten of himself walking into the police station.

Paint had been used to draw a red circle on his back. Special care had been taken to make the circle look like the crosshairs of a rifle. But that wasn't what worried him. What worried him were the words, also in red, painted across the bottom—CONFESS OR ELSE.

The meaning was clear. Whoever had sent this to Bex wanted her to confess or they would kill Max. It didn't take a genius to know what they wanted her to confess—that she'd killed Bobby Caldwell. He turned the envelope over.

"No stamp. No return address." He looked at the bodyguard. "Were you on duty when the mail came?"

"No."

"It doesn't matter who was on duty," Bex said. "I wasn't home when the mail came. I was running errands."

"And the bodyguards are watching you, not your house," Max said.

"Exactly," she agreed.

Footsteps sounded off to Max's right. The chief was heading toward them.

Bex sighed. "That picture is karma I suppose, telling me it's time to face my past." She laughed nervously.

Max's gut clenched with dread. This was suddenly one conversation he did not want to have with a station full of cops listening.

"Miss Kane," the chief said as he stopped beside Max. "Thank you for finally coming in. Let's go right to the interview room. We have a lot to discuss."

She swallowed and looked past him to the room at the front left corner of the station, a wide window clearly showing the table and chairs inside. "O-okay."

Thornton smiled like a Cheshire cat and crossed the room. He held the door to the interview room open and waved his other hand for Bex to join him.

She started toward him.

"No." Max stepped in front of her, blocking her way.

She frowned. "Max, it's okay. This is what I expected to happen. I can't hide from the past forever. I need to tell you what happened the night that—"

"Shut up, Bex."

Her eyes widened with surprise.

"Now listen here," Thornton half shouted from across the room. "Sounds like Miss Kane has important information pertinent to our investigation. You need to be very careful about what you're doing, son."

Max ignored his boss. He frowned down at Bex. "You need to go back home. Now."

She shook her head, apparently trying to be brave even though she was trembling. "I can't. You're in danger. Don't you see? And it's my fault. I have to tell you what I—"

"Not one more word." He grabbed her hand and hauled her toward the exit.

Chapter Fourteen

Bex stared through the windshield of Max's truck as he raced down a gravel road, far faster than she'd have dared but somehow managing to maintain complete control. The truck stayed smoothly on the road, without those scary slides toward the ditch that always happened when she went over thirty on one of these back roads.

"I don't understand," she said. "You've been trying to get me to go to the station for an interview and the moment I do, you practically kidnap me to shut me up. And then send my bodyguard away."

"I'm your bodyguard now. I'm protecting you from yourself."

He slowed the truck, then turned down another gravel road, this one even more narrow than the last. If they came across someone coming the other way, she had no idea how they'd pass each other.

"Max, where are we going?"

In answer, he slowed even more and waved his hand toward the windshield. The trees thinned out and gave way to a wide expanse of cleared land with only an occasional shade tree dotting the rolling hills. Winter grass was coming up new and thick, turning the dried brown summer grass into a gorgeous green swath of color. And on the top of the hill a football-field length away was an impressive-looking log cabin. The front was dominated by a large glass A-frame in the middle and a covered porch that appeared to run all the way around the cabin. The roofline was irregular, pitched sharply in places, hinting at massive open spaces inside.

He pulled his truck up in front of the porch and killed the engine.

"Yours?" she asked.

"Yep. Let's get inside before this storm breaks."

She leaned forward, peering up at the dark clouds swirling overhead. Before she'd even managed to open her door, Max was lifting her out. She put her hands on his shoulders until he set her on her feet, then quickly stepped away, trying not to think about how good it had felt to be in his arms again.

"I could have gotten down by myself." She motioned toward the metal steps on the side of his truck.

"I know." He directed her up the porch steps and followed behind.

Feeling his gaze on her, her face flamed with heat and she found herself wishing she'd put on something nicer than a pair of jeans and a plain white blouse. And that, in turn, had her angry with herself for caring about her looks, and Max, when that was the last thing she should be thinking about right now.

She stopped at the glass door set into the wall of A-shaped glass that allowed her to see into the expansive two-story foyer and main room. The back wall was A-frame glass, too, with an even more breathtaking view of a gorgeous lake and the rolling hills beyond.

"What an incredible home. And the view is amazing."

He unlocked the door and shoved it open. "I like it."

"Like it? This is paradise." She hurried inside, drinking in the warm golden tones of the log walls, the soaring ceiling with its massive beams. The circular metal chandelier entwined with deer antlers, suspended from a heavy chain in the middle of the room. The furniture was dark brown leather with metal beading. Chunky wooden end tables and a massive coffee table took up the rest of the sitting space in the center, with lots of open floor surrounding them. The whole place was incredibly masculine, elegant in its simplicity, uncluttered.

As he took their jackets and hung them on hooks beside the door, she said, "This place suits you. It looks like you made all your dreams come true—working as a cop, having a gorgeous piece of land away from town. I'm happy for you."

He cocked his head, studying her. "What about you? Did your dreams come true?"

The only dream she'd ever had was to spend her life with him. She stepped away from him and stood looking out the back wall of glass at the water, beaten into small whitecaps by the wind.

The sound of clinking glass had her glancing over her shoulder. Max stood at one end of the room, pouring drinks at a bar built out of what appeared to be old barn wood, stained honey gold like the rest of the cabin.

He joined her by the windows and handed her a glass. "Something relaxing, like old times. Still like bourbon and Coke?"

She smiled and took it from him. "Still do. Even though I wasn't even legal drinking age back when we shared a few of these."

He leaned against the wood frame, facing her. "There were a lot of things we did that we shouldn't have back then. Our parents would have been furious if they knew."

She almost choked on her drink, coughed, then

gave him a watery smile. "Don't you know it. My mama would have killed me if she realized half the nights I was supposed to be staying with a friend I was sneaking out to be with you."

His brows raised. "You really think your mom didn't suspect what was going on? I practically lived at your house, we spent so much time together. You don't think she figured out you were sneaking out to be with me the rest of the time?"

She shrugged. "She was a smart lady. I suppose she might have known and turned a blind eye. She loved you like the son she never had. You won her over just like you won…" She stopped and shook her head.

"Just like I won you over?" he said.

She nodded, seeing no point in denying it. How could she? She'd loved him since she was twelve or thirteen.

He sipped his drink, his gaze never leaving her face. He took both their drinks and set them aside on the brick hearth of the fireplace not far from the doors. Then, very slowly, he leaned down, giving her every chance to turn away, and he kissed her.

She closed her eyes, melting against him, her arms, as if of their own will, sliding up his chest to wrap around the back of his neck. He cupped her head, his other hand caressing her back, his thumb tracing little circles against her skin through the thin fabric of her blouse.

The kiss wasn't rushed or frantic as many of their kisses had been when they were teens. This kiss was more of an exploration, more of a question, hesitant but confident, if there was such a thing. It was as if he wanted her to give him the green light or tell him to stop. There was heat, but it was carefully banked. A fire ready to burn, but ruthlessly held back. All it did was frustrate her and leave her wanting more.

She broke the kiss and shoved out of his arms. She gave a nervous laugh and retrieved her glass from the hearth.

"Will you have to confess to one of your interns that you kissed me? I'd hate to get in the middle of a happy couple."

She downed the rest of the drink in one swallow, then had to swipe at her eyes when the burn had them watering.

"I wouldn't have kissed you if I was still dating someone else." His tone was clipped, his eyes cold.

She regretted her words as soon as she'd said them. Apparently Marcia's earlier gibe about Max and interns had struck deeper than Bex had realized. Not that it should matter. Max wasn't hers, could never be hers again. She needed to remember that.

She moved into the kitchen, separated from the living area by a black granite–topped island. After washing her glass out in the sink, she set it on the drain rack to dry.

"You didn't need to do that," he said, his voice quiet but the deep timbre carrying easily through the massive space.

She shrugged and crossed to one of the couches. Worried that he might sit beside her, she chose one of the recliners instead, kicking off her leather loafers and pulling her legs up. "You didn't need to bring me out here to talk, either. I could have done my talking at the station. All you did was delay the inevitable."

He set his glass down on the coffee table and sat on the end of the couch closest to her. "What's inevitable?"

She rubbed her hands up and down her arms, even though she wasn't cold. "The inevitable is that you'll just have to take me back to the station again."

"Why? So you can confess to something you didn't do, just because you think you're protecting me?"

She shook her head. "No, Max. I would confess to something that I *did* do, in order to protect you. I'm guilty. I killed Bobby Caldwell."

Chapter Fifteen

"I don't believe you," Max said.

Bex stared at him. He was calmly sitting on the couch, proclaiming his belief in her innocence.

"I thought you'd be shocked, or angry, or… something, when I finally confessed. I didn't expect you to refuse to believe the truth."

"Oh, I believe that you believe you killed him. That's something I suspected all along. It explains why you wouldn't see me when the chief threw you in jail. It explains why you left town the first chance you could. And it also explains why you stayed away so long. But do I think you could actually murder someone? Not a chance in hell."

Her fingers curled against the arm of the chair. "So, what, I hallucinated the whole thing? Some cop you are. The guilty party confesses and you ignore the confession."

He let out a deep sigh. "Bex, something awful happened to you after you left me that night. I think Bobby was probably stalking you again, maybe he lured you somewhere, or forced you to his cabin. He tried to rape you, maybe he did rape you—"

She shook her head. "No."

His jaw tightened and he nodded, a look of relief flashing across his features. "But he attacked you. And you fought back. If he died as a result of that, it was self-defense. Not murder."

Unable to sit still, she jumped to her feet and began pacing across the room. "It's not that simple." She rubbed her hands up and down her arms. "Yes, Bobby tricked me into going to his cabin that night. Yes, he attacked me, and I fought back. I may not have meant to kill him, but I did." She stopped pacing. "Self-defense?" She laughed bitterly. "Of course it was. But who would have believed me?"

"I would. I do. I would have helped you, if you'd given me a chance."

"All that would have done was destroy your dream to become a police officer. Thornton wouldn't have overlooked that you were siding with me. Trust me—he believes I'm a murderer, and he believed it back then, too."

"That's because you wouldn't talk. You refused to say anything in your defense."

"I couldn't. You know how things were. Bobby had been stalking me and making my life hell.

But he was too clever to do it in front of others where I'd have proof. He manipulated everyone into thinking I was the crazy one making up stories about him. His father would have painted me out to have been the one to lure him to that cabin. And he would have said that I did that in order to kill him for making me look like a fool. He was rich enough, and blind enough when it came to Bobby, to make everyone believe him. I'd have gone to prison for the rest of my life. That's why I couldn't tell anyone. My only hope to avoid prison was to keep my mouth shut and hope that there wasn't enough evidence to prosecute me."

"Then why confess now?"

"You know why. Someone—probably Bobby's father—is trying to bring up the past, make me face what happened. If I don't—"

"They'll kill me? Good grief, Bex. I'm a police officer. I know how to take care of myself. I don't want you to be a sacrificial lamb on my behalf, especially when you're innocent."

She crossed her arms. "Am I innocent if I was glad he died? Because I am. That sounds terrible. And I've felt guilty for years over not feeling guilty about that, if that even makes sense. I know I shouldn't be relieved that someone lost their life. But Bobby was sick, evil. And I know that he would have killed me eventually if he hadn't died that night."

He stood and stepped in front of her to stop her pacing. Then he put his hands on her shoulders, making her face him.

"You have nothing to feel guilty about. Looking back, with my years of experience behind me, I've no doubt that you're right. He would have killed you eventually, or tried to. But I would have protected you, Bex. If you'd only let me."

She blinked away the moisture that was suddenly in her eyes. "I told you it's not that simple. It never was."

He tilted her chin up. "Because you wanted to protect me. Don't you realize it's my job to protect you, not the other way around?"

She shook her head. Because he was wrong. Bobby's friends had beaten up Max more than once in that terrible year when Bobby was harassing her. It was only a matter of time before something terrible happened to Max. And it was her fault, for somehow drawing the attention of someone like Bobby. She couldn't let Max pay the price for her failures.

"Bex," he said, his deep voice soft, but with a thread of steel underlying it that hadn't been there when they'd been teenagers. "There's absolutely nothing to gain at this point in bringing any of this up now. Leaving town like you did back then was like running away. It only made you look guilty in the eyes of most. And it makes claiming self-defense this many years later extremely hard to prove. Which is why you have to be quiet. No confessions."

She shook her head. "We both know I can't just go back to Knoxville and pretend none of this happened. As soon as I came to Destiny, I started something. And whether it's Mr. Caldwell, or someone else behind what's happening now, they aren't just going to stop."

"All right. Then there's only one thing we can do. We have to investigate Bobby Caldwell's death on our own and get the evidence we need to prove you're innocent. Then, and only then, we'll go to the chief and present our case." He dropped his hands from her shoulders. "Wait here. I'll be right back."

He left before she could argue again and headed through an opening at the far right side of the room, near the kitchen. His boots echoed on the hardwood floor. A few moments later he returned with what appeared to be the same thick manila folder he'd brought to her house last night. He also had a legal pad and pen.

He plopped the pad and pen on the end table beside him and put the folder on the coffee table. Sitting on the edge of the couch, he flipped the folder open and sorted through the various papers and pictures. He finally found whatever he was looking for, a page with a graph of dates and times with bulleted sentences next to each time. He tapped the page.

"I've got the official timeline surrounding Bobby's death right here, the record of what he did the entire day until a specific time, and then later when his body was discovered by Deacon and his father."

A chill passed through her at the thought of the father and son finding Bobby's body. That had to be a nightmare they'd never gotten past. And from the hate and bitterness she'd seen in the senior Caldwell at the lawyer's office, he'd definitely never moved past his son's death.

"I've read everything in this file dozens of times over the years. So I'll know if your story jibes with what we know or not."

She blinked again, surprised. "Why did you read it dozens of times?"

"The woman I loved ran away. What do you think?"

She shrank back from the bitterness in his tone. "I'm sorry, Max. I truly am."

"Meaning if you could do it over again, you wouldn't have told me no when I asked you to marry me that night?"

"I didn't say that."

"Exactly. Then you aren't truly sorry, are you?"

She winced. "If we're going to fight, maybe

you should just take me back to the station and let me get my confession over with."

He closed his eyes briefly, then shook his head. "No fighting. I'm…sorry, Bex. Seeing you again after all these years has been a huge shock. Apparently I'm not taking it very well."

She swallowed hard and nodded. "Me either. I never know what to say around you without making you upset. That's why I didn't go to your mom and dad's when I got in town. I would have loved to say hi to your family. But I didn't want to risk upsetting you after the way I left things between us."

He stared at her incredulously. "You wanted to see my family, but, what, you were trying to run in and out of town purposely not trying to see me?"

"I'm doing it again. Everything I say comes out wrong. Can you please just drive me to town, Max? Neither of us is doing each other any favors here."

"Sit down, Bex."

The bite in his tone had her sitting before she even thought about it. Then she got so mad at herself for following his directions that she jumped up and started past him toward the front door.

He stood and grabbed her arm, stopping her. "Bex—"

"No." She shook her hand, but his fingers remained around her wrist, like an iron band. Tears burned at the backs of her eyes and her breath started coming in gasps. "Stop it, Max. You don't have the right to tell me what to do or keep me from leaving if I want to leave. Don't you get it? That's what he did. He'd corner me in some alcove at school, or surprise me in my own backyard when Mama wasn't home. And he'd scare me, use his superior strength to try to make me do what he wanted. He'd grab my arm, just like you're doing now."

His eyes widened and he immediately let her go. The blood drained from his face as she rubbed her wrist.

"Bex, my God, I'm so sorry. I wasn't thinking about…about what you went through." He held his hands up and took a step back. "I won't physically try to stop you from leaving. But please, please think about what you're doing. I want to help you." His eyes took on a tortured look. "I couldn't protect you back then, even though I tried. But I'm a grown man now. And I know what I'm doing. Let me protect you now. Let me keep you safe."

His phone buzzed. He frowned and checked the screen, then flipped a button on the side to silence it.

"Bex? What's it going to be? Will you let me help you?"

She couldn't bear to see the hurt in his eyes, hear the hurt in his voice, knowing she was the cause. No matter what she did, she always seemed to hurt him. Ever since he'd asked her to marry him and she'd turned him down. Her entire life had turned upside down after that. And now she was turning his upside down, too. What would have happened if she'd said yes?

No, she couldn't go down that road. She couldn't have said yes back then. No matter how much she loved him, she'd known that if she said yes, she was signing his death warrant. Because that was one of Bobby's many taunts to her—that if he couldn't have her, no one would. And she believed him. He would have killed Max if she'd agreed to marry him. And that was something she couldn't bear.

True to his word, Max wasn't trying to stop her by using his physical strength against her. Because he wasn't Bobby. Max was a good man, always had been. And it was wrong of her to ever compare the two.

"I'm sorry," she said. "I shouldn't have said that, about Bobby, and you…it was cruel. And a lie. Because I know you would never hurt me. You're nothing like him, Max. You never were, and never will be. You're the most decent man I've ever known."

He gave her a tight smile. "I don't know about

that. But I do know I want to help you. Will you let me, Bex?"

She slowly nodded. "If I can. What do you want me to do?"

"I need you to tell me exactly what you did the day Bobby Caldwell died, from the moment you woke up until the cops knocked on your door around one in the morning." He grabbed the legal pad and pen and sat down on the couch, waiting.

"But…you know most of it. We were together until around nine thirty that night." She didn't meet his gaze. She couldn't. Because that was when he'd asked her to marry him. And she'd turned him down.

"All of it," he repeated, not missing a beat. "From your perspective, from the moment you woke up."

She let out a deep sigh and sat beside him, pulling her legs up on the couch to get more comfortable. At least, sitting here beside him, she didn't have to look into his eyes while she recounted the more intimate details.

"Mom woke me up, as she often did. I've never been much of an early riser. But it was my birthday, and a Saturday, and she knew I didn't want to miss a single minute. We had a lot of plans."

"We who?"

"We, Mom and me. And then…you and me."

She cleared her throat. "We were supposed to meet later."

He hesitated for just a moment, then said, "Go on."

She described the day of shopping with her mom, going to a nail salon to get matching manicures and splurging on pedicures, too, at the last minute. Her mom was a retired schoolteacher, having had Bex late in life as a surprise baby. So she had a lot of free time, but not a lot of money. But she'd promised Bex an eighteenth birthday to remember and had saved all year for it. Nothing was too good for her Bexey.

She plucked at the fabric of her pants. "I'd forgotten that nickname until now."

He put his arm around her, pulling her close. "I'm so sorry about your mom."

She blinked back the moisture in her eyes. "Thank you. I'm glad you were there for her. She…spoke about you a lot. She loved you very much."

He squeezed her shoulders. "Do you need to take a break?"

"No." She wiped her eyes. "I want to get this over with." It took a minute to get her bearings. Then she began telling him about the rest of her day with her mom. Buying matching purses at one of the little stores in town that had hand-crafted items Bex always thought were way better than anything she'd ever seen in any fashion magazines. Lunch at her favorite restaurant, a seafood chain the next town over.

"That was pretty much it. I spent my daylight hours with Mom. Oh, she also made homemade strawberry cheesecake and we stuffed ourselves with a piece of that when we got home. Then she gave me a kiss, we hugged, and she gave me her car keys so I could go see you."

"You left the house around what time?"

"Seven thirty, give or take. I drove straight to the barn at the edge of the Caldwell property, just a stone's throw from where your daddy's land began. You were already there."

His fingers idly rubbed her shoulder through her blouse, but he didn't say anything.

She sniffed, wiped her eyes again. "It was the most romantic evening we'd ever had. You thought of everything. You had fresh hay strewn all over the floor with soft blankets and pillows. Lanterns cast a soft glow."

He let out a puff of laughter. "We're lucky we didn't roast alive with all that flammable fuel. I don't know what I was thinking."

"You were thinking that you wanted my eighteenth birthday to be perfect. And it was. And so was your proposal. I'm so sorry that I ruined everything, Max."

His arm dropped from around her shoulders

and he made a few notes on his pad, as if she hadn't just mentioned the moment when she'd destroyed their future. But she could tell from the lines of tension on his forehead that he wasn't as immune to the memories as he pretended.

"We left at the same time," he said. "You in your mom's car, me hoofing it across the field to go home. That was about nine thirty. I had to get up early the next day so my dad could help me rebuild the carburetor in the old junker we were restoring together. But you didn't go straight home, did you? You were seen later that evening in town. With Bobby."

She stiffened beside him. "I wasn't *with* Bobby. I was never willingly with Bobby. Ever."

He tilted her chin up. "You don't have to tell me that. I knew firsthand how obsessed he was with you, that he wouldn't leave you alone. I fought more than one fight with him and his father's hired hands out at the farm trying to get him to leave you alone. So don't get all upset like you think I'm implying something when I'm not. He was a sick stalker. Period. But because of the crappy laws, there wasn't anything Thornton could do until Bobby actually crossed the line and hurt you. It sucks, it really does. But that's how it was back then."

She blinked against the burn of unshed tears and let out a shaky breath. "I know. I'm sorry."

"Stop apologizing, Bex. Let's just try to stop doing things that hurt each other and get through this, okay?"

"Okay." She settled back against the couch. A burst of lightning lit up the darkening sky. The water behind the house was so choppy now that it reminded her of the rapids in the creek that ran behind the Caldwell property, gouging deep cliffs thirty feet and higher, hidden from the Caldwell mansion by a copse of thick trees. Cliffs she and Max and a group of other teens had climbed a dozen times on dares, until the farmhands that doubled as Robert Caldwell's security men had chased them off with guns one night.

They'd all been fools and were lucky to be alive. She had never understood why old man Caldwell felt he needed all those thugs around him. But maybe that kind of paranoia came with being wealthy. Then again, he did have a spate of vandalism one year, some neighborhood kids spray painting his barns with sexually explicit cartoons. It was funny until he produced footage from some hidden cameras on the property and was able to get those kids thrown into juvie for their crimes. So maybe he wasn't so paranoid after all. Maybe he was the smart one.

"Go on," Max encouraged. "You left the barn at nine thirty. Then what happened?"

"When I went into the house—"

"You went directly home?"

"Yes."

"What time was it when you got there?"

"I drove straight from the barn to the house, so that probably took about fifteen minutes. And I was only home a few minutes, like maybe ten. Mama was on the verge of one of her migraines. I think we overdid it—maybe she was dehydrated from drinking too many sodas while we were out, I don't know. Anyway, she was out of pills. I got back in the car and drove into town to the only twenty-four-hour convenience store, on Maple Street and Fifth."

"Smiths."

"Yes."

"I remember looking up at that huge clock above the door and it was 10:22."

"Ten twenty-two exactly?"

She nodded.

"How can you be so sure?" He scribbled down the time.

"I remember saying to myself that if something horrible happened to me that night, I needed to tell the police it happened at 10:22."

His gaze shot to hers. "Why would you think that?"

"Because that was when Bobby Caldwell walked into the store."

Chapter Sixteen

Bex twisted her hands together, the bad memories washing over her from that awful night ten years ago.

"He harassed me, as usual. Grabbed my arm, rubbed up against me."

Max's pen stopped, his knuckles whitening around his pen. "Was anyone else in the store?"

"The sales clerk. I don't know his name. Oh, and Marcia."

"Marcia Knolls?"

She nodded. "She was following Bobby around as usual. And he was ignoring her, bothering me instead. I told him to leave me alone and I hurried to the register to buy Mama's pills. After paying, I ran out to my car and left."

"Where were Bobby and Marcia at that time?"

"Marcia came out shortly after me, drove off in her car. I remember she ended up behind me at a stoplight and gave me the finger. I didn't see

Bobby come out of the store. I'm not sure where he went right after that."

"You drove straight home?"

She shook her head. "No. I realized I was almost out of gas and was worried I wouldn't make it home, so I stopped and filled up." She told him which station she'd used.

"Did anyone see you?"

She waved toward the manila folder on the table. "If that's the case file, don't you know this part? I'm sure the chief had his men comb the town to create a timeline for his persons of interest. And with me as the number-one suspect, you probably know exactly how many gallons of gas I got and how I paid for it."

"I knew you were at the store and got gas. But I didn't have your side, that Bobby was harassing you. And I didn't know Marcia was at the store. I'm not trying to be cruel by taking you through every step. I'm just trying to ensure that we don't miss anything, okay?"

"Okay."

"You filled up, went inside to pay?"

"Had to. I didn't have Mama's credit card, didn't expect to need gas. She only gave me five bucks for the pills. Luckily I had some of my babysitting money in my purse. But, yeah, I had to go inside to pay. Mr. Alverson was the one working that night. That one's easy to remember. He's there all the time. Even now. I saw him there last week."

Max's mouth quirked in a half smile. "He runs that place like his own little fiefdom. How long were you inside?"

"Not long. Maybe five minutes. I drove home, gave Mama the pills, put her to bed. I was about to go to bed myself when I heard a soft knock on the door. But no one was there. That's when I saw the note. Someone had slid it under the door."

He stopped writing. "A note? Who was it from?"

"You."

His head jerked up. "Me? I didn't send you a note."

"I know that now, of course. The note was supposedly sent through one of your friends. It said your dad was mad at you for something and took your phone. But that you really needed to talk to me, that it couldn't wait. I figured you were still angry at me turning down your proposal, that maybe you were going to try to convince me to say yes. But I was also worried that something else had happened, that maybe you were in trouble. The note said to meet you at a cabin on the Caldwell property. It even had a little hand-drawn map."

"You didn't think that was odd? You didn't think to call me?"

"Why would I? I had no reason not to believe the note, that your dad had your phone. We'd met in that barn on the Caldwell property a dozen times. I figured the cabin was somewhere new you'd discovered, yet another building close to the border of your dad's property where we could meet without being caught. It really didn't seem any different than meeting you in our usual spot. And, well, after we'd left on such bad terms, I figured maybe you didn't want to meet at the barn. Karma and all that. I was anxious to try to smooth things over. I didn't want you to hate me."

A pained expression crossed his face. "I could never hate you, Bex. I assume that was the same cabin where Bobby's body was later found?"

She nodded.

"Please tell me you kept the note."

"I had it with me when I went to the cabin. But not when I left."

"I didn't see it listed in the police report of items found."

"All I know is that it was in my pocket when I got there. But not later. I assume Bobby took it."

He set his pen and notepad on the end table and turned to face her. "Tell me everything, Bex. Exactly as you remember it."

"As soon as I got there and went into the outbuilding, I knew I'd been tricked. You weren't there waiting for me. Since your house is so close by, there's no way I'd have gotten there before you. I turned around, and Bobby had just come inside. He was grinning like an idiot as he closed the door. But I was the idiot." She clenched her hands into fists.

"What did he do?"

She closed her eyes, wishing she could block out the memory of Bobby just as easily. "He threw me to the floor and…and lay on top of me. He held my face still and kissed me. When I tried to bite him, he squeezed my jaw until I cried out. I didn't try to bite him again. It was awful. He ripped my shirt, sending buttons flying all over the cabin. He had a knife. He cut my bra off. And then, then he…" She shook her head. She couldn't tell Max all the horrible things that Bobby had done to her, how he'd held the knife to her and put his mouth where Max's had so recently been. It was like he'd destroyed every beautiful touch she and Max had shared before he'd asked her to marry him, and then turned it into something ugly.

"Earlier, at your house when I first questioned you, you said he didn't rape you. Was that true?" His voice broke on the last word, and she realized this was just as hard for him as it was for her.

"No. No, he didn't…penetrate me. After he tore off my clothes and did his worst, he was about to…and I knew I couldn't live with myself if he did. I couldn't get my knees up to kick him, so I…" She shuddered. "I grabbed him…there…and squeezed as hard as I could. He screamed and fell off me. I scrambled to my feet and he was calling me ugly names and I'd just reached the door when he grabbed my hair. He yanked me back and I remember I flailed my hands out for something, anything to stop him. And I grabbed something off one of the shelves. Later, I realized it was an empty wine bottle. Probably from the last kids who'd snuck onto the farm and used that cabin. I swung it around in an arc. There was a horrible, sickening thud. And then he fell down on the floor. Dead."

Tears were flowing down her face now. "I gathered up my clothes, searched for the buttons, but I couldn't find the last one. I couldn't stay another minute, knowing he was dead. So I ran, got in the car. Drove home. And that's why my mama wouldn't let me talk to the police. She knew what I'd done the moment I got home in my torn clothes. She burned them in the fireplace. She vacuumed the car, scrubbed it down, just in case I'd brought any evidence back with me. And she burned the vacuum bag, the paper towels she used, everything. And she made me swear never, ever to say anything at all to the police."

She was crying hard now, and hated that she was crying. And suddenly Max was in front of her, kneeling on the floor. He'd scooted the table out of the way and was pulling her hands down from her face, looking up at her with some kind of emotion she couldn't even fathom.

"Are you absolutely sure you told me everything from that night? You didn't leave out any details?"

"The only details I left out were the vile things he did to my body before he tried to rape me. No, Max. There's nothing else to tell. I killed him. I didn't mean to, but I did. And Mama and I were both too afraid to say anything because I'd made so many complaints about Bobby. And his father always made the complaints go away. And everyone knew I hated him. There was no way they'd believe me over Bobby's father."

She drew a shaky breath. "I'm not a complete idiot. When I was in jail, after the chief locked me up, I had plenty of time to sit and think about what had happened. And I knew that Mama and I had made some really bad decisions. Maybe if we'd called the police right away and didn't burn my clothes, the clothes might have helped build my case of self-defense. It's possible, I suppose. But by then, we'd already destroyed evidence. Even at eighteen I knew that was wrong, illegal and only made me look guilty. I couldn't tell the chief what really happened at that point. He could have arrested my mom for helping me cover up what happened."

She could tell from the intensity of his gaze and the way he was looking at her with laser like focus that she wasn't going to like his next question.

"Bex, you said you wouldn't let me see you in jail, to protect me. Because you were worried that it could hurt my future career aspirations. While I might not agree with your decision, I can sort of understand it. At that age, as young as we both were, I get how things could look different. But when the chief didn't have enough evidence to press charges, you left town. And you stayed gone for ten years. Why, in all that time, did you never once call me?"

And there it was. The question she'd both expected and dreaded ever since she'd come back to Destiny. It was one of the primary reasons she'd hoped to avoid him. She twisted her hands in her lap, and said the only thing she could think of.

"You didn't call me, either."

His brows raised. "You made it painfully clear through Chief Thornton that you never wanted to see me again. I respected your wishes, even if I didn't understand them."

She looked away.

"Bex. Why?"

She squeezed her eyes shut, swallowing hard

against the tightness in her throat before looking at him again. "Everything just sort of built on everything else. After what happened with Bobby that night, I knew that if I let you back into my life you would do everything you could to protect me. If I spoke to you, I knew I'd tell you exactly what I did, what my mom did to help me cover it up. That would make you complicit in destroying evidence and would ruin your future career. Whether you agree with my reasons or not, all I can say is that my life became a snowball that kept rolling downhill and getting bigger and bigger. I left town to let things die down, hoping Mr. Caldwell would quit lobbying for me to be arrested. Mama kept me updated on what was happening with the case and I knew it only got worse after I left. For a long, long time Mr. Caldwell pushed and pushed the chief to find and arrest me."

Max slowly nodded. "You're right. He was like a crazy man for the better part of a year before he stopped visiting the station every day, demanding your head on a silver platter."

"I know. And by then, I was building a life in Knoxville. I had the antique business going. And from there, it was easier if I didn't think of Destiny and what I'd run from."

"Including me?"

Her lip wobbled when she answered. "Yes. Including you. It hurt just to think about you. You were the reminder of everything that I'd lost. It was easier to push you to the back of my mind. To try to never think of you again."

He winced and looked toward the back wall of windows at the ever-darkening stormy-looking sky. What had he expected her to say? That she loved him then, loved him still? She did, with her whole heart. But she'd lost everything the night Bobby Caldwell died, including Max. And the only way she could survive that loss was to start over.

A long time passed in silence. When Max finally turned back toward her, he was Detective Max again. All business and professional. With none of the earlier warmth he'd shown. He asked her more questions, and every time she heard his cold voice, her heart broke a little bit more.

Finally, after answering another one of his questions, she said, "This is such a nightmare."

His jaw tightened, and she knew he was probably thinking the same thing. Except that his nightmare was that he had agreed to help her. And that he was most likely regretting that decision now.

"Just tell me one more thing," he said. "Do you remember if Bobby wore his ring that night?"

"The chunky one with diamonds all over it, the one his father gave him as some kind of heirloom? That he lorded over all of us at school? That ring?"

"Yes. That ring."

"Definitely. It got caught in my hair when he grabbed me. Ripped out some of my hair by the roots. Or, at least, it felt like it."

"Did you take the ring with you when you left?"

"No. I wish I'd thought to. It probably has my DNA all over it, from my scalp. Yet another reason not to cooperate with the police. Why? I'm guessing you found it and want me to give a DNA sample for comparison?"

He shook his head. "The ring was never found."

She frowned. "But that doesn't make sense. He was definitely wearing it."

"You said you hit him on the head with a wine bottle?"

"Yes. It was one of those blue ones. I don't remember the label."

"What did you do with the bottle?"

She frowned again. "Other than hit him? Nothing. I already told you what happened."

"Humor me. Please. Did you take the wine bottle?"

"No. I didn't take anything but the buttons from my shirt, the ones I found anyway. The note that was in my pocket was gone. All I can figure is when Bobby was…pawing me, that he yanked it out. Probably to make sure I couldn't show it to anyone to prove that he'd lured me there. I didn't think to look for it when I left, because I didn't know it was gone at the time."

"Did you clean the cabin?"

She gave him an incredulous look. "I just told you I didn't take anything or even stop to see if I still had the note."

"Bex. It's important. Did you clean the cabin?"

"No. No, I didn't clean the cabin. I was too messed up to even think about something like that. I grabbed the buttons that I saw, grabbed my clothes and just…ran, back through the trees to where I'd hidden my mom's car."

"Are you sure about these details? You've told me everything?"

"I've been seeing that same night play out in my nightmares for ten years. I'm sure."

"Bex, if you're telling me the truth—"

"I am. I swear."

"If you're sure you've told me everything, then I'm sure of something else. You absolutely did not kill Bobby Caldwell."

Chapter Seventeen

Bex stared at Max in disbelief. "Don't give me the usual cop platitudes of self-defense and yada yada yada. I'm telling you it doesn't matter. No one would believe me any more today than they would have back then. They're going to put me in prison, so I might as well get used to the idea."

"I'm not giving you platitudes. You didn't kill Bobby."

She frowned. "What are you talking about?"

"When you left the cabin, I promise you, Caldwell was very much alive."

"But...the police found his body a couple of hours later, when his father and brother went looking for him."

"Yes. But the most you did was knock him out for a few minutes. That wasn't what killed him. Bobby died from internal bleeding, a ruptured spleen."

"I don't…understand. How is that possible? When I hit him, he fell so hard that his spleen ruptured?"

He shook his head. "No. That wouldn't have done it. Someone beat him. They took a baseball bat or something like that and hit him across the lower back and abdomen. The coroner counted at least a dozen blows. They beat him, left him there to die. And then they took his ring. His father reported it as missing in the police report, said Bobby never went anywhere without it. That means that after you left, someone else went inside that cabin and killed him. There's no other explanation."

"I didn't kill him," she said, in wonder.

"No. You didn't." His smile faded. "But right now all we have is your word. And, unfortunately, if you tell anyone else what you just told me, it only corroborates that you were at the murder scene."

She blew out a frustrated breath. "No telling what physical evidence your boss has that ties me to that cabin. I imagine he found my missing button. There had to be hair, too, and fibers from my clothes that he tore."

"No. There isn't. That's one of the reasons that Thornton never could get a judge to sign a search warrant for your home. That cabin was pristine. Like someone had scrubbed it down top to bottom that night. There was no blue wine bottle. No button, no hair or fibers. And no note, either."

"Why? Why would someone do that? Do you think they saw me go into the cabin and wanted to…what, protect me from being blamed?"

"Possible. More likely whoever killed him just wanted to clean every inch of the place in case any trace evidence could be used against them. I think they took advantage of the fact that you'd knocked Bobby woozy and they decided to finish him off. Then cleaned up afterward so no one would know they were the one who'd killed him."

Her earlier elation faded. "So I did kill him after all. I left him there, semiconscious, unable to defend himself."

"Don't start feeling guilty over his death now. You said it yourself earlier. Bobby Caldwell was a bad person. He was the worst kind of scum, someone who preyed on women. The only person Bobby can blame for what happened is Bobby."

His words made sense. She'd accepted long ago that she'd killed him, and didn't feel guilty for that. But now, knowing that she'd left him injured, easy pickings for someone else to kill him, she did feel guilty. It was an odd feeling, to finally have compassion for a man she'd hated all of her adult life.

"What do we do now?" she asked.

"We go over your story again, from beginning to end."

"What? Why?"

"I need to know every single detail that you can remember. Someone out there, whether it's Bobby's father or someone else, believes you killed him. And they're determined to get you to confess. If there's anything else that you can remember about that night that I can use to help your case, and put the true murderer away, then going over and over your story will be worth the pain."

He grilled her about every single detail that day. He even made her recount as much as she could remember about the week leading up to Bobby's death, looking for anything that might give them a clue about who else might want Bobby dead. He took mercy on her well past the lunch hour when her stomach started rumbling. But after they wolfed down ham and cheese sandwiches and potato chips, he was back at it.

"What about after Thornton released you from jail?"

Bex was lying on the couch now, her head propped on a throw pillow and one arm thrown over her face. Mad Max, as she was beginning to label him in her thoughts, was currently perched on the edge of the coffee table beside her, pen scribbling after every question he asked her.

She wanted to grab that pen and snap it in two.

"What about when I got out of jail?" she asked wearily without moving her arm.

"You were in town for two weeks, rumors swirling around, people saying terrible things. And all the while, Bobby's family was making things really difficult for you, demanding the chief arrest you."

"No, not his whole family," she said. "Just his parents." She lowered her arm and rolled her head on the pillow to look at him. "I never did hear how the father ended up in a wheelchair. And I haven't seen Mrs. Caldwell in town since I got here. Were they in a car accident or something?"

"Worse. She died of breast cancer earlier this year. A few months later, he was diagnosed with late-stage bone cancer. His bones are so brittle he was walking down the sidewalk one day and his hip just snapped. That's why he's in the wheelchair. They say he doesn't have long to live, maybe a few months, best case." He straightened and frowned off into the distance.

"Max? Something wrong?"

He slowly shook his head. "No. I need to make a phone call. Hang on a sec." He grabbed his phone and punched in a number. A few moments later he said, "Hey, Colby, yeah, it's me. Mmm-hmm. Mmm-hmm. I figured he'd be ticked. That's why I ignored his earlier calls. Nothing I can do about that right now, but I'm still working the case. I need to ask you something. Remember when Mrs. Caldwell was being treated for cancer, where did she go for that? Uh-huh. And Mr. Caldwell, he's been going through chemo at the hospital. But I never asked which one. I just assumed Maryville. But where…" His gaze shot to Bex as he nodded. "Right. Got it. That's what I was thinking. Did Blake make any headway with his contacts? What about your interviews?"

Several minutes later, he hung up the phone.

"Well," she asked, "do I have to beg you to tell me what that was all about?"

He smiled. "That was Colby, one of the other SWAT guys who's also a detective like me."

"I know who Colby is."

"Right. Well, he reinterviewed two of the gunmen at the hospital. One of them, a guy named Lenny, finally admitted that he'd seen the guy who hired them to go after you. He worked with an artist to do a rendering of the guy."

"It can't be Robert Caldwell if he's in a wheelchair. He couldn't drive."

"It wasn't. But close."

"Deacon? He's such a nice guy."

"No, it wasn't Deacon. The picture is the spitting image of one of the security guys Caldwell senior keeps at his farm. Even more importantly, the new guy on our team, Blake, was able to link that car to that security guy. It sure looks like he was the one in Knoxville who hired those thugs to go after you. And it's not like he had that kind of money, or a motive. Only his employer had that. Even better, Mr. Caldwell—the father, not Deacon—was quite familiar with Knoxville, since he and his wife were both there most of this year for cancer treatments."

"Okay, sounds like he's probably the one behind going after me. At least now we know who it is."

His confidence seemed to take a tumble. "Well, I'm not sure about that. Yes, he's the one who hired the gunmen, through his personal security guy. We should be able to prove that after we get a warrant for his bank records and follow the money. But what's his motive? He believes you killed his son and he wants you to confess. He wants you to go to prison because he thinks you're a murderer. That's problematic."

"I really hate that I see where you're going with this," she grumbled. "Your point is that the current bad business between Mr. Caldwell and me makes it seem highly unlikely that he's also the one who killed his son. Because if he'd done that, he wouldn't dredge all of this back up right now and shine light onto it."

"Exactly. Now you're thinking like a cop."

"Lord help us all."

He laughed, but quickly sobered. "Who does that leave us, suspectwise? I'm thinking we're back to Marcia Knolls."

"Marcia? But she was in love with Bobby. She wouldn't want to kill him."

"He wasn't in love with her. He treated her like an insect he wanted to brush off his shoe. You said yourself that you saw her in the store that night with Bobby. Maybe she followed you and you didn't know it. And after you ran out of the cabin, holding your clothes, she thought you'd actually been his lover and were running home, maybe to make curfew. I can see her justifying it that way, and being angry and hurt and going into the cabin to confront Bobby. When she found him lying there, unconscious, assuming he was naked—"

"He was." Her voice was so tight she could barely speak.

"Okay. He was naked, and she thought he was cheating on her, at least in her mind. So she grabs whatever is handy. Cabin like that, on the edge of the woods, there's bound to be stuff in there, maybe in a closet. A bat or something like it. She could have hit him with it while he was still unconscious, so that even if he woke up while she was hitting him, he'd already be too hurt to put up much of a fight." He pulled out his phone. "The more I think about it, the more I'm convinced she's the only one who makes sense for Bobby's murder. I'll get Colby to bring her in for questioning."

A few minutes later, he hung up the call and pitched his phone onto the coffee table. "Okay, I put everything into motion that I could. Hopefully the guys will come through for us and get proof and wrap it all up."

She eyed him with dread as he picked up the legal pad and pen again. "I thought we just solved the case. Marcia killed Bobby. And Caldwell senior had one of his men hire the thugs to get me to confess. Why are you getting your torture devices out again?"

He rolled his eyes. "Because I still want to review the two weeks you were in town after Thornton let you go. I want to know who all you spoke to, and what they said. Who you might have seen skulking around. Until Colby tells me that he has Marcia's confession, I'm not letting down my guard. We need to see if anyone else around town did anything odd those two weeks that might make them rise to the top of my suspect list for having killed Bobby."

She groaned and collapsed back onto the pillow.

Chapter Eighteen

Max rubbed the back of his neck and looked out the wall of glass to his deck and the angry, broiling sky over the lake beyond. The sun had set long ago, but the frequent cracks of lightning illuminated the heavy clouds that had been threatening rain most of the day. He figured the storm would finally let loose its full fury and drench them with rain soon. But until then, it was doing its best to whip the last of the dry leaves from the trees, making winter look even closer than it was.

A snuffling sigh sounded behind him and he turned around to see that Bex had fallen asleep on the couch while he'd taken a few minutes to stretch his legs. He was tempted to smile at the adorable picture she presented. But he didn't really feel like smiling. It was hard to when the woman he'd loved had rejected him so soundly all those years ago, and then put him out of her thoughts for ten years. He sure as hell hadn't put her out of his.

In the beginning, he'd been pathetic, begging her mother to tell him where Bex had gone. Later, once he'd become a cop and knew how to find her, he'd tracked her down. He'd driven to Knoxville and planned on confronting her. By then, he was well past the blubbering love-struck fool phase. He'd lived in the anger phase for a good year or two. And he wanted to demand an explanation. But when he'd seen her, he couldn't do it. Couldn't go up to her and debase himself to ask her why she'd left. Ask her why she'd never called. He was too angry to even form a coherent sentence.

After that, he'd never gone to Knoxville again. And he'd almost convinced himself that he'd forgotten her until she'd shown up at that deli counter. And just like that, all his old feelings of anger, grief, resentment had risen to the surface and formed a crack in the heart he'd thought he no longer had. And in just a matter of days he'd brought her to his home and begged her to tell him why she'd never tried to see him, talk to him, after she left.

He was such a fool.

He strode to the couch and looked down at her. But the anger and resentment faded away, replaced by a pathetic longing that went deep in his soul. Bex. His Bex. She would always be his in his battered and bruised heart, even if not in reality. No matter how much he wished he didn't care about her.

Her exhaustion was evident in the dark circles under her eyes. She needed to sleep. But he still had some questions. And he imagined his boss would be parked at his doorstep early in the morning, demanding that he get his butt back to work and bring Bex with him.

On the outside, Thornton was a grumpy pit bull. But when it came to his team, he was often full of bluster. He considered the SWAT team his family, and because of that he'd forgive Max the sin of ignoring his orders and walking out of the station with Bex. But Max knew better than to push it a second day. That would cross the line. He'd be suspended at best, fired at worst. Being a cop was something he'd wanted for as long as he could remember.

But what he'd really wanted, more than anything else, was lying on his couch, a thin line of drool drying at the corner of her mouth.

God, she was beautiful. Maybe not in the classic way most men thought of beauty. She had short legs, her mouth was wide, her cheeks round—something that had always bothered her, especially in middle school when other kids had called her chipmunk cheeks. She'd practically starved herself in eighth grade trying to get the narrow, thin face she thought she should have until she'd made herself sick. She'd finally had to realize that no matter how thin she was, her face never would be. Max liked to think that maybe he'd helped her with that, by telling her how beautiful she was, over and over, until she started to believe it.

He hadn't been lying. He really did see the beauty others missed. It came from inside and shined through her bright, curious, intelligent eyes. The silky hair she despaired of never holding a curl was a wonder to him, soft as a rabbit. Those legs she thought were too short were perfectly proportioned to her body. She looked like one of those Disney fairies. All that was missing was a set of wings and a wand. She already possessed the magic, because she had utterly enchanted him.

She snuffled again, grumbling something in her sleep as she scrubbed at her mouth. Then she rolled over toward him. And opened her eyes.

He crouched down, almost at eye level. And his heart ached. "Hello, beautiful."

Her eyes blinked. "Don't call me that. I must look terrible." She covered her face with her hands.

He gently pulled them down and, despising

his inability to resist her lure, pressed a soft kiss against her lips.

Instead of kissing him back, she shoved at his chest and hurriedly sat up, covering her mouth and mumbling something behind her hand.

She was so cute when she was half-asleep and still confused.

"Betghrm," she mumbled behind her hand again.

He tilted his head. "Hard to be sure, but I think you might be asking about the bathroom?"

She nodded enthusiastically.

He held out his hand. "Come on. I was going to question you some more, but I think I'll give you a reprieve. You're too far gone to make sense anyway. I'll show you the guest room."

She hesitated, then put her hand in his and let him pull her to standing. She let his hand go and stepped back, running her hands through her hair as if worried about her appearance.

"I'll just freshen up and then you can drive me home."

"I'd rather you stayed the night."

She frowned. "Why?"

"You mean other than the fact that the wind is whipping and dry lightning is cracking outside?"

Her gaze went to the windows. "I must really be tired. I hadn't even noticed."

"Even if it weren't storming, I'd strongly suggest that you consider staying. Whoever is after you knows about your mom's house. I can protect you here, if it comes to that."

She ran her hands up and down her arms and nodded. "Makes sense. Thanks. I appreciate it."

"No trouble at all. The guest room's the first one down the hall on the left. There are toothbrushes, shampoo, everything you need in there. Oh, except something to sleep in. My room is right next door. You're welcome to grab one of my T-shirts to sleep in if you want."

"Sounds good." She grabbed her purse from one of the end tables and started toward the hallway, then stopped. "Max?"

He'd just rounded the island going into the kitchen but waited and raised a questioning brow.

"Thank you," she said. "For everything. I know we haven't figured out how to clear my name yet. But for the first time in, well, forever, I feel like there's hope. So, thanks."

"You can always count on me, Bex. I'm always here for you. No matter what." Sappy, but true. No sense in denying it.

Her eyes widened, and then she whirled around and disappeared down the hall.

Max let out a deep breath and headed into the kitchen. They'd talked right through dinner and his stomach was rumbling. He grabbed a handful of grapes from the refrigerator and leaned against the counter, popping them into his mouth and chasing them with a bottle of water. When he finished his snack, he headed into the main room to kill the lights.

Was Bex asleep already? Probably. She'd seemed so worn out. He couldn't help smiling, thinking about her lying in the middle of the bed, wearing one of his T-shirts. He froze in the middle of the room, his smile fading. His T-shirts. He'd told her to grab one. He kept them in his top dresser drawer.

But that wasn't all he kept in that drawer.

He swore and flipped off the main light then hurried down the hallway. The light was on in the master bedroom, streaming into the hall. *Hurry. Stop her.* He bolted to the doorway then froze. Bex was standing in front of the dresser, her hair freshly brushed, but still wearing her jeans and blouse. One of his T-shirts dangled from her left hand. Maybe he'd caught her in time.

Her eyes slowly rose to his, and then she held up her other hand, the one holding a diamond solitaire ring.

BEX'S WHOLE BODY shook as she held the same ring that Max had offered her so long ago. There was no mistaking it. Every facet had been branded into her memory. It was definitely the same ring.

"Why?" she asked, her voice barely above a whisper. "Why did you keep it?"

His jaw tightened and he crossed the room to her, swiping the ring from her palm and grabbing the little black box from the drawer full of T-shirts. "No reason, just never got around to returning it." He shoved the ring back in its velvet bed and popped the lid shut.

"It had to have cost a small fortune. You probably made payments on it for years," she said. "You couldn't have forgotten it."

His expression was shuttered, remote, as he faced her. "I believe that you have everything you need in the guest room. Have a good night's sleep. I'll see you in the morning."

"Oh, Max. What have I done?" she whispered. Hot tears traced down her cheeks.

He let out an impatient breath and strode to the door, holding it open. "Good night, Bex."

Like two duelers at ten paces, they faced each other—her with his T-shirt clutched in her hand, him with the promise of forever in his. A promise he'd once offered out of love and she'd refused, also out of love. But he didn't understand that. She'd never explained any of that to him. And seeing the ring in his drawer had shocked her to the core, and made her realize for the first time that maybe she'd been wrong. She'd made a decision to protect him. But she'd also shut him out, never explained her reasons, and left him in a state of limbo, always wondering *why*.

This amazing man in front of her deserved so much better than that. She wasn't the girl she'd been back then. She was a grown woman. And it was high time she came clean about everything, not just the horrible events around Bobby's death. She needed to explain to Max why she'd told him no.

She slowly padded toward him in her bare feet and lifted his hand away from the door.

He frowned down at her, obviously not sure what she was doing. She smiled sadly and pushed the door closed.

A wary look came over him. "Bex, what are you—"

She pressed her fingers against his lips, startling him into silence. "I owe you an explanation, for this."

She tried to take the velvet box, but he pulled it back, a gentle tug-of-war.

"Please," she said. "I don't deserve your trust, but I'm asking for it. Trust me. I'll just put this back in the drawer."

Without a word, his back so stiff he could have been a soldier submitting to inspection, he relinquished his hold on the box.

Unable to resist another look, Bex opened the

lid and turned it, watching the solitaire twinkle beneath the overhead light.

"Bex—"

"I know, I know. Sorry. It's just so beautiful." She slowly closed the lid and replaced the box in the drawer. After tossing the T-shirt onto the king-size four-poster bed, she crossed to Max again and took his reluctant hand in hers. "Can we sit down, just for a few minutes? I need to tell you what I should have told you years ago."

The struggle inside him was evident in the expressions on his face. Unlike a lot of tough guys, Max didn't do stoic very well. He was tough, yet sensitive, always caring. It was one of the things she'd always admired about him, one of the reasons she'd known he'd be an excellent cop—because he cared.

Although the master bedroom was large, it was neat and sparse, like the rest of the house. There was only one chair, on the right side of the bed. So she tugged his hand, urging him toward the bed with her. She let his hand go and had to climb up on the blasted thing, it was so high. Then she turned around and patted the spot beside her.

He looked like he was trying not to laugh, and finally gave in to a grin. "You look like Tinker Bell climbing up on that bed."

She shook her head. "I never did understand your fascination with fairies."

"Not with fairies. Just you." His smile dimmed and he sat beside her. "Whatever you think you need to say, you don't. I don't have any expectations of us getting back together. There's no reason for you to feel uncomfortable or worry that I'm going to hit on you."

"You kissed me in the family room."

"Momentary insanity. I recovered. It won't happen again."

She looked down at her hands, trying not to let him see that his words had struck their target. Her heart. She braced herself and forced herself to look up, not to cower and not to run again when the going got tough.

"It's time I faced my past," she said. "I've already told you about the night of my birthday in regards to Bobby Caldwell. But I didn't tell you everything, not the part about us."

He swallowed, his Adam's apple bobbing in his throat. "You don't have to do this, Bex. It really doesn't matter anymore."

"It does matter. I hurt you, and that was never my intention, in spite of how it must have seemed. All I ask is that you listen. It won't take long. I just want to explain why I said no."

He shrugged as if he didn't care. But his gaze was riveted on her and he didn't protest anymore.

"You'd been hinting about that night for a while, talking about how special it would be, how important it was. It didn't take a genius to figure out you were probably going to propose. We'd certainly talked about the possibility of spending the rest of our lives together often enough. I think we both always assumed we'd end up together. I certainly thought I'd be your wife one day, that we'd build a life together, create our own little family."

His breathing hitched, but he didn't move, just kept watching her.

"I don't know if you remember, but Chief Thornton had come to the school earlier that week for one of his career day speeches. And just like every year before, you hung on his every word. And after it was over, you talked about your big dream, of being a police officer here in Destiny, of being a detective and working your way onto the SWAT team. It's the only dream you ever really wanted."

His jaw tightened, but again he said nothing.

She sighed. "Anyway, I knew how important that was to you. And I also knew that if that dream was ever taken away, it would utterly destroy you." She twisted her hands in her lap. "You'd already gotten in trouble fighting Bobby many times to try to protect me. That was okay while you were still a minor. But you turned eighteen two weeks before I did. If you fought Bobby again, you could have been charged as an adult.

And that would have given you a criminal record. I couldn't let that happen."

He frowned. "Bex—"

"Wait. Let me finish. There's more to it than that. I was afraid for your life. The situation with Bobby kept getting worse, and I didn't know what was going to happen or what to do. All I knew for sure was that Bobby was winning the war. And he was evil and told me many times that if he couldn't have me no one would. If I had married you, Bobby would have killed you. I know it. I couldn't live knowing that I had caused your death."

He stared at her incredulously. "You told me no because you thought I couldn't protect myself?"

"What? No, I mean, yes. But you make it sound so simple. It wasn't. I truly thought Bobby would kill you if I didn't end things between us."

Tears splashed down her cheeks onto her hands. She impatiently wiped them away. "But even if I was wrong, if Bobby tried to hurt you and you ended up killing him instead, that would have destroyed you just as completely. Because it could have destroyed your dream of becoming a police officer. What if you were convicted of manslaughter or something like that? Thornton wouldn't have allowed you on the police force with a record. I couldn't let that happen. I couldn't live with myself knowing you'd grow to hate me a little bit every day we were together, realizing that I was the reason you'd given up what you truly loved."

His hand firmly tilted her chin up so she'd look at him. The anger that flashed in his eyes startled her.

"Are you saying you turned down my proposal to protect me? Either from Bobby or from myself?"

She tried to nod, but couldn't, so she whispered, "Yes."

He swore and stood up, his boots ringing against the floor as he paced in front of the bed like a caged tiger. "All this time, I thought maybe you'd played me. That you didn't really love me."

She blinked in shock. "I've always loved you."

"Funny way of showing it."

"I know. I'm so sorry. I never meant to hurt you."

He stopped pacing in front of her. "You may have loved me, but you sure as hell didn't know me."

"Excuse me?"

He braced his hands on the bed on either side of her. "Do you honestly think that being a cop was my biggest dream? That what I truly loved, more than anything else, was the idea of being a detective and a SWAT officer? Sure, I wanted to be a cop. And I wanted to stay in my hometown to do it. But a career wasn't the love of my life. You were. I'd have given everything I had for you and never regretted it for a single second. Ten years, Bex. For ten years I've been asking myself what I did wrong, what was there about me that made me unworthy of you. I couldn't figure it out. I thought, maybe, one day, if you ever came back, you'd tell me about this horrible thing that I'd done to you and it would make the lightbulb click in my mind. I'd be like, *oh, wow, that's what I did.* And then I'd apologize and do everything I could to make it right. But I didn't do anything wrong."

He thumped his chest. "I did everything I could for you, loved you with every ounce of my being. And you didn't love me enough to even have a freaking conversation over your fears so we could work through it. You know what, Bexley? If you'd just asked me what I wanted, I'd have told you that we could move away somewhere, start over in another town. I'd have gone anywhere, done anything and been happy, as long as I was with you. Instead, you didn't trust me, or love me enough to give me a chance. You didn't give me my dream by leaving me. You stole my dream, Bex. Because being a cop wasn't my dream. Being with you was."

He whirled around and strode out of the room, slamming the door behind him.

Chapter Nineteen

Bex's mouth fell open, Max's angry words repeating themselves in her mind as the sound of his boots rang through the house. Wind suddenly howled outside the bedroom door, followed by a metallic thump. He'd gone outside, in the middle of a lightning storm. Because of her.

Oh, God, what had she done?

She shoved off the bed, hopping down to the floor just as the lights flickered and went out. Letting her memory of the house's layout guide her, she flung the door open and ran down the hall into the main room. She froze at a loud pinging sound against the glass.

"It's just the storm." Max's deep voice spoke from the dark. "It's finally raining. The wind is driving it in sheets against the back of the house."

She turned toward his voice, but the room was too dark to make out anything but silhouettes. He was standing by the fireplace, one of his booted feet resting on the raised hearth, a hand braced against the mantel.

She turned, looking for one of the lamps she'd seen earlier.

"Don't bother." He spoke from the gloom again, his voice already drained of anger, sounding flat, emotionless. "The power just went out."

She started toward him, then let out a curse when her shin banged the coffee table.

"Wait there," he said.

He bent down, but she couldn't tell what he was doing. Light flared, like from a long match. Then a small fire began to grow in the fireplace. He must have had it set up with kindling and logs, ready to go, because it quickly caught and grew into a roaring fire. The flames threw a flickering, eerie light across his features and through the room.

He turned his back on her. "Go to sleep, Bex. The house is sturdy. You don't need to be afraid of the storm."

The coward inside her, the one who'd never picked up the phone or tried to talk to him for all those years, urged her to do as he said. But coming back to Destiny had changed her irrevocably, had reawakened feelings long ago buried, had made her realize just how her actions had impacted those around her. Running away, going back home without making things right, wasn't something she could do now. She had to face what she'd done. All of it. And that meant facing Max one more time.

She circled the coffee table and crossed the room to stand directly behind him.

"Max, you didn't let me finish explaining why I told you no."

He sighed wearily. "I've heard enough."

"Maybe you have. But there's one more thing I have to tell you. It might not matter to you. But it matters to me. I realize how much I've hurt people by leaving when I did, by running away. And I'm trying to make it right the only way I know how, by telling the truth. There might not be any proof of what really happened that night with Bobby. But when this storm is over and the sun comes up, I'm going to call the chief and tell him to come get me so I can give a full statement. Because it's not just about me. It's about Bobby's father, and his brother. They deserve to know what I know. Someone killed their loved one that night, and they need to know my role in it, if nothing else, so they can expend their energy looking for the right killer."

He turned his head, hand braced on the mantel, boot still resting on the hearth. But at least he was listening.

"I already explained why I turned down your proposal," she continued. "But I didn't explain why I left. Bobby was dead. So there wasn't any worry by then that you'd get in trouble fighting or going after him."

He frowned. "I wondered at that, after I left the bedroom."

The fact that he was at least talking with her now gave her hope. She plodded forward. "I left because I thought I'd killed Bobby. I've thought that all this time, until you proved to me today that I didn't kill him. I left because I knew that if I stayed in town, you would do everything you could to help me. And I wouldn't be strong enough to resist you for very long. I talked it through with Mama and we both agreed, the only way to protect you was for me to leave."

He shook his head in disgust. "There you go talking about protecting me again. Don't you realize that's my job? To protect you?" He looked back toward the fireplace. "Or it would have been. If you'd stayed."

"Exactly."

He frowned and looked at her again.

"That's my point," she said. "You would have felt it was your duty to protect me, even after I'd turned you down. Because that's how you are, a wonderful, good, loyal, kind man who would protect the woman he loved even if she was a murderer. Even if it cost him his career."

He swore again. "We're right back where we

started. Bex, you're way more important to me than any job. Don't you get that?"

"Actually, yeah, I do. Now. You've ignored your boss's calls all day and risked everything to be here with me, to keep me from confessing back in town. You're doing exactly what I tried to prevent by running away in the first place."

He shook his head.

She stepped closer, placing her hand on his chest, feeling his muscles bunch beneath her fingertips. "But I'm not running this time. I'm not going anywhere. I love you, Max. And we're both adults now. I don't know if you can ever forgive me for not trusting you and giving you the chance to make your own decisions about your future all those years ago. But I'm hoping you can at least try."

His gaze dropped to her hand. "It's been a long time, Bex. A lot has happened since then. I don't know that I want to go down that same road, risk you crushing me like you did. It took me years to get over you. But I'm happy now. I like my life, enjoy my family, this house, the life I've built. I'm not sure you fit in anymore."

She smoothed her hand over his shirt, her hand shaking, sadness welling up inside her. "I'm not asking you to fit me back into your life. I'm asking you to work on trying to forgive me. And then maybe we'll see where we go from there."

Slowly, as if he wasn't sure what she'd do, he moved his left hand toward her face, then gently stroked her hair back, feathering his fingers through the strands.

"Still as silky as ever," he whispered.

"Still so handsome you can stop a girl's heart with one look," she whispered, smiling up at him.

His mouth twitched. "That handsome, huh? Sounds dangerous."

"You have no idea." She moved closer, until her breasts pressed against his ribs.

His lids lowered to half-mast. His hand shook as he continued to stroke her hair. "I don't think this is a good idea, Bex. We haven't settled anything at all between us."

"You're right. Nothing's settled. But we've had an incredible run. And I can't think of a better way to say goodbye—if this is goodbye—than to share ourselves with each other one last time. It sure beats how we ended things last time. How *I* ended things. Let's write a better ending to our story than walking away from each other angry and bitter. We deserve that. Max and Bex deserve that. Don't you think?"

In answer he groaned and yanked her to him, his mouth slamming down on top of hers. Heat filled her, warming her from the inside out. She struggled to get closer to him, standing on her tiptoes. He lifted her with one hand beneath her bottom, setting her feet on the edge of the hearth, the roaring fire warming her back, Max warming everything else.

This kiss was nothing like the one he'd given her earlier. That one had been distant, questioning. He'd held back. He wasn't holding anything back this time. And even though she'd always thought they had something special between them, comparing everything before to this was like comparing a candle to an out-of-control wildfire.

Thunder boomed overhead. Lightning lit up the house like broad daylight. But it barely registered in her mind. There was only room in her thoughts for Max and how he made her feel. She twisted against him, her tongue tangling with his, her fingers sliding down between them, eagerly working at the buttons on his shirt.

Groaning deep in his throat, he lifted her again, striding across the room to the big leather couch. He gently lowered her back onto the cushions, following her down, down until his delicious weight pressed against her. Every inch of her body was plastered to his, and it felt so good she stretched, rubbing the side of her calf against his hip as they kissed and kissed and kissed. It was as if they were trying to catch up on every moment they'd lost in the years they'd been apart. And neither of them could bear to stop long enough to shed a single item of clothing.

Desperate for more, she reached between them and fumbled with his belt. She managed to get his jeans unzipped, and then she slid her eager fingers inside. His entire body shivered as she filled her hands with him. He broke their kiss, gasping for breath, already rock hard, his hips jerking against her.

Then he was sliding his own hands down her body, and they were like two frantic teenagers all over again, working at each other's jeans, only managing to get half-undressed before he was poised at her entrance, pushing against her.

He swore and pulled back.

She wrapped her knees around him, trying to pull him down again.

He laughed, his harsh breath rasping against her ears. "Hold it. Just give me a second, sweetheart."

The sound of foil tearing jolted her out of the haze of passion enveloping her. A condom. Had he kept it in his pocket? That thought had her remembering the interns he'd dated and she stiffened beneath him. But then he was pressing against her again and all her jealousies evaporated beneath the need to have him inside her, filling her. She'd wanted this for so long, with him, and nothing was going to spoil it.

And then he was inside her, and it was even more wonderful than she'd remembered. Her body knew Max's, yearned for his, as if they'd been made for each other. Every thrust was met with an answering arch of her hips, heightening her pleasure, making his heart gallop faster in his chest where it pressed against hers.

He braced his forearms on the cushions, keeping the full weight of him from crushing her as he made love to her. And she took full advantage of the space between them, sliding her hands up beneath his shirt, relearning his contours, every muscle, every dip. She wanted to slide down his body, taste him, stroke him. But that would have to wait. The delicious things he was doing to her, his clever fingers caressing her as he thrust inside her, were bowing her body back against the couch.

Panting, she drew her knees up on either side of him, twisting, arching, her fingers curling on the leather couch as she strained with him to reach that pinnacle of pleasure she knew was waiting for her.

He leaned down and captured her mouth with his, his back arched, his hips bucking against hers. And then, with one clever stroke of his body and his hand, she came undone in his arms, crying out his name as she exploded in a shower of ecstasy around him.

His powerful body thrust into her several more times, wrenching every last bit of pleasure from her that he could, all while he worshipped her mouth with his. Then he stiffened, his body spasming inside hers as his own climax washed over him. His fingers tightened on her bottom, clinging to her as he spent himself. And then, ever so slowly, like embers from fireworks floating to the ground, he lowered himself to the couch, turning with her in his arms.

They lay there, holding on to each other tightly, their hearts racing, breath coming out in harsh pants until their bodies began to cool and they could once again breathe without rasping.

She kissed the base of his throat, and he whispered romantic words in her ear, making her hot all over again. A few minutes later, he left her long enough to clean up. She should have gotten up, too. But she felt like her bones had turned to water and couldn't bring herself to do more than pull up her panties and jeans and collapse back onto the couch.

Then he was there, fully clothed again, like her, pulling her into his arms as he cradled her against his chest on the couch.

"I'll carry you into the bedroom when I get

my strength back," he promised. Seconds later, he was softly snoring.

She smiled, then closed her eyes and joined him.

THUNDER BOOMED OVERHEAD, startling Bex out of a deep sleep. She jerked upright in the dark, confusion clouding her mind as she tried to remember where she was. Lightning streaked across the sky, illuminating the family room for a brief second. She let out a breath of surprise. She was on the couch. But Max wasn't with her. Had he gone to bed and left her there? No, as soon as that thought occurred to her, she pushed it away. He was probably in the bathroom, or maybe in the kitchen getting a late-night snack.

She swung her legs over the side of the couch and stood, expecting to see him standing on the other side of the island, maybe grabbing a couple of beers out of the refrigerator.

"Max?" She squinted in the dark. "Where are you?"

He didn't answer.

"Max?"

She felt her way through the house, checking the three bedrooms, yanking blinds open so the moonlight and lightning would help her see. One of the bedrooms was set up like an office. But she didn't find any sign of him. Worry began to coil in her stomach. She tried a light switch, but the house remained dark. The power was still out. Maybe he was in the garage, checking the fuses. Yes, that made sense. That's what she'd do if the power was out.

She hurried through the family room to the left side of the house, which boasted a powder room, a laundry room and a three-car garage. Lightning flashing through the glass panes in the garage door showed her that he had a Jeep parked inside. But there was no Max to be seen. Where else could he be?

Real fear began to gnaw at her. She ran back into the family room, turning in a wide circle.

"Max, where are you? This isn't funny. Max?"

Again, nothing.

Had he gone outside in this wretched storm? She couldn't think of any reason for him to do that. But maybe he liked watching the rain. Her mom always had. Yes, that was it. There was an enormous wraparound porch on the front and sides of the house. She ran to the door and jerked it open. The front porch was empty, except for some man-size rocking chairs on either end.

"Max," she yelled out into the yard. "Where are you?" The wind seemed to capture her words and snatch them away.

His truck remained parked just a few feet from the steps. Empty.

Panic had her fairly flying through the house again, checking every room, every closet, even looking beneath beds. Finally she stopped in the middle of his bedroom. She had to acknowledge what she'd been trying to avoid all along. He was gone. Something must have happened to him.

She couldn't fathom what that might be. All she was sure of was that he must be in danger. And she needed help to find him. She ran back into the main room and grabbed her purse to get her phone. But her phone wasn't there. She frowned. Had she left her phone at her mother's house? She couldn't remember the last time she'd seen it.

A landline. There had to be a landline in the house somewhere. No, she hadn't seen any phones either time she'd run through the house. What was she supposed to do now? Lightning lit up the back wall of windows again, illuminating the back deck. Could he be out there? It was the only place she hadn't looked.

She ran to the sliding door. The storm was getting worse, blowing rain in great sheets. She peered out at the darkness.

Thunder boomed overhead, and a brilliant flash of lightning lit up the deck before plunging everything into darkness. Wait, something was off. What had she seen? She leaned forward, peering in the moonlight. Part of the deck seemed charred. From the lightning? It flashed again, and she let out a startled scream. There was a large handprint on the glass. And it was covered in blood.

Chapter Twenty

Rain whipped at Max's face like dozens of icy-cold needles pricking his flesh. The ground was turning to mud, making the field treacherous and hard going. Lightning flashed overhead. He instinctively ducked down, not that it would have done him much good if the lightning had been close enough to hit him.

"Stop stalling. The cabin's straight ahead. Move."

He looked over his shoulder. The long bore of the rifle pointed steadily at him, but too far away for him to have any chance of knocking it down.

"Move," Marcia repeated, shouting to be heard above the storm.

"Drop the gun," he called out to her. "You haven't shot anyone yet. You can still get off without much jail time, maybe only probation."

She laughed bitterly. "I'm not going to jail. And

if you want your girlfriend to live, you'd better get moving."

He clenched his fists but started forward again. Just ahead, the silhouette of a familiar cabin loomed in the dark. The same cabin he'd seen in dozens of crime-scene photographs, the one at the edge of the Caldwell property where it joined his father's, and now his, as well. The cabin where Bobby Caldwell had been killed ten years ago.

And now Max knew who'd killed him.

He stopped at the door and glanced back. "Now what?"

Marcia motioned with her rifle. "Go inside and shut the door behind you."

Something metallic flashed in the moonlight just over Marcia's shoulder. She stiffened, then very slowly raised her hands in the air. The person behind her yanked the rifle away and shoved her toward Max. Lightning flashed again, illuminating the man behind her.

Deacon Caldwell, holding a wicked-looking knife.

He shoved the knife into the top of his boot and straightened, the rifle pointed at Marcia now.

"You okay, Detective?" he called out.

Max looked at Marcia, who was glaring at Deacon.

"I'm fine," Max yelled back. "Thanks to you. Follow me back to my house and I can handcuff her and check on Bex." He grabbed Marcia's arm and yanked her toward Deacon.

When they reached him, Deacon was shaking his head. "Too far. This lightning's getting too dangerous to be outside. My house is much closer, and I've got a generator. We can call the police from there."

Another bolt of lightning struck close by, the thunder boom almost right on top of it. Sparks showered down from a nearby tree.

Max swore, the hairs on his arms standing up from the electricity in the air. "That was close. Where's your house? I thought you lived with your father?"

He motioned toward the trees on the other side of the cabin. "Straight through there. I had it built for when I got out of the military. Close enough to help my dad when he needs me but not so close that I give in to the urge to strangle him." He grinned. "You know how families can be." He waved at the cabin. "The roof's gone on that, no shelter there. My house is the only place that makes sense. Let's go."

He headed past Max, going at a fast clip toward the trees.

Max hesitated, looking up the hill that would lead him back to his house. He hated leaving Bex alone. If she woke up and saw the charred wood on the deck and his bloody handprint on the glass—both courtesy of Marcia's sick plan—she'd think the worst. What would she do then? Especially since Marcia had forced Max to take his and Bex's cell phones and toss them into the lake?

"He's waving at us," Marcia grumbled beside him, tugging at her arm to get him to let her go.

He tightened his grip. "Come on." He hurried after Deacon, pulling Marcia with him.

As soon as they rounded the copse, the lights from a two-story house came into view. Deacon was right, his house was much closer. He was standing on the porch already, waiting for them.

Max bounded up the steps, pulling Marcia with him. When he reached the top, he shook his head. "It's a monsoon. Can't believe we were out there in that."

Lightning flashed again, thunder cracking overhead.

"It'll play itself out soon if you believe the weatherman. Come on in. The mudroom's on the right. We can dry off there."

The three of them sloughed off the rain with a handful of towels as best they could, then they headed into the main room of the house.

Max directed Marcia to a chair beside the couch. "Sit down. Don't make me chase you. I'm mad as hell at you and won't take kindly to having to run out in that storm after you again."

She rolled her eyes and plopped down, crossing her arms and promptly ignoring both of them.

"Mad as a hatter," Deacon said.

Marcia glared at him, then turned away.

Max shook his head. "I don't think Marcia's insane. I think she knows exactly what she's doing. She must have planned this from the moment she saw Bex and me in town."

"What exactly did she do?" Deacon asked.

"Set my back deck on fire, for starters. I saw flames flickering outside and ran out to see what was going on, thinking lightning might have hit something close by. She was waiting right outside the sliding glass doors with her rifle. The rain put the flames out pretty quick and she poured a bottle of blood onto my hand and made me press it against the glass. Bex is going to think the worst if she wakes up and sees that."

"It was possum blood. But your girlfriend won't know that. She'll think you got hit by lightning and you're done for. It'll be nice for her to be scared for a change, for her to see how it feels to have someone you love die," Marcia said.

"That was your plan?" Max asked. "To kill me in that cabin? Like you killed Bobby?"

Her eyes widened. "I didn't kill Bobby. Bex did."

Was Deacon right? Had Marcia lost her sanity and convinced herself she hadn't done what was now obvious? He studied her carefully as he said, "Bex didn't kill Bobby."

"Oh, please. Everyone knows she did."

"I'm afraid that's my fault," Deacon said, sounding regretful. "I allowed everyone to think that for so long that after a while it seemed more like fact than conjecture."

Max grew very still and turned toward Deacon. "What are you talking about?"

The rifle in Deacon's hand lifted, pointing straight at Max's gut. "I think it will be better if I show you. Marcia, be a dear and get the DVD out from beneath the TV over there, the one on the bottom in the red case." He shrugged. "Red seemed only fitting. Makes it easy to find, too."

Marcia hesitated, looking confused.

The rifle swung toward her. "Hurry up," Deacon ordered. "Knowing dear old Dad, he'll make one of his men bring him over here to check on me in this storm. Not because he gives a damn but because the chosen one is long dead and I'm the only heir he has left." His mouth twisted in a sneer. "I'd rather have all of this over with before he does. It will be easier that way."

"What will be easier?" Max asked, taking a step toward the other man.

"Don't," Deacon said, aiming the rifle at him again. "I don't want to hurt anyone. Don't force my hand. All I want you to do is watch a movie. Marcia, if you please."

She pressed a button, and a black-and-white picture displayed on the TV. Max recognized it immediately.

"That's the interior of the cabin where your brother was killed."

"Yes, it is. Father is a bit obsessive about security. He has cameras all over the place. Imagine my surprise when I discovered he had one at the cabin. Thank goodness I was smart enough to look for it. This is the recording from that day. Oh, I have to warn you. Parts of it might be hard for you to watch, Max. And the end, Marcia, I guarantee you won't appreciate that part. But I'm looking forward to our little movie night. I've been wanting to set the record straight for some time now."

The door opened on the screen.

"Ah, here we go," Deacon said. "Too bad we don't have popcorn. Ah, well. It's not like I planned this for tonight. When I saw Marcia out skulking around the property, I had to act fast. But I'm rather good at making the best of a bad situation. You'll see."

Max clenched his fists at his sides as, on the screen, Bex entered the cabin. There was no sound. But he could see the puzzlement on her face as she looked around. And he could clearly read her lips as she apparently called out, "Max?"

"Isn't that sweet?" Deacon said. "She's looking for her lover, for Max. Marcia, you'll want to pay particularly close attention to this next part. You've convinced yourself that Bobby loved you, that he wasn't using you for sex every time he went after his primary target and failed. I mean, come on, Marcia. Did you really think Bex wanted Bobby? He was a slimeball. He stalked her for months. And every time someone saved her from his clutches, he'd run to you so he could pound out his frustration inside your body. That wasn't love, my dear. That was abuse. The man was sick."

Marcia stood off to the side, her face pale from both Deacon's words and the tableau playing out on the screen.

Max wasn't doing much better himself. He was sick to his stomach seeing Bobby surprise Bex in the cabin, then throw her to the floor, pawing at her and forcing her to suffer his groping hands all over her body. If Bobby Caldwell had been alive today, Max would be hard-pressed not to kill him himself.

"Turn it off," Max ordered.

"And miss the best part? I think not." He winced. "Oh, that had to hurt."

On the screen, Bex had just smashed a wine

bottle against the side of Bobby's head. He dropped to the floor like a stone.

Marcia keened an animallike cry between her clenched teeth.

"Oh, good grief," Deacon said. "Even after seeing her supposed boyfriend trying to rape another woman, she's still upset over him getting hurt. You really need professional help, Marcia, love."

Max had a pretty good idea that Deacon was the one who needed professional help. All these years he'd thought Bobby was the only crazy one. Apparently the crazy gene ran in the family.

As Bex ran out of the cabin on the TV, Max inched his way toward Deacon, very slowly so as not to draw his attention.

Deacon stared at the screen, his eyes lit with a half-mad light. "And now, folks. We've finally reached the good part."

Max looked at the screen. A man wearing a dark jacket with a hood over his head entered the cabin and bent over Bobby. He slapped Bobby's face several times. Bobby winced, then his eyes fluttered open.

"Ah, there, you see?" Deacon said. "Bex didn't kill my brother after all. That's what I wanted you both to know. Now watch very closely."

It didn't take long. The man in the cabin, with his back to the screen, was apparently arguing with Bobby. Bobby shoved him out of his way and headed for the door. The bat seemed to come out of nowhere, swinging right for the middle of Bobby's back. His body slammed against the door and plopped down onto his back on the floor, a trickle of blood dribbling out from the corner of his mouth. The bat slammed down again, this time on Bobby's stomach. Again and again it came down. Bobby raised his hands to protect himself and rolled over, trying to push himself up. The bat came down once more, twice, and then Bobby was still.

Max stared in horror at the screen. Marcia had covered her mouth with her hands. And then the hooded man turned around, looked directly up at the camera, and smiled.

The same smile Deacon Caldwell was giving Max.

"Now you know," he said, sounding as if they were discussing the best crops to plant next spring, his voice relaxed and upbeat.

They were in big trouble.

Max glanced at Marcia, then toward the French door behind her. She gave him a subtle nod, letting him know she understood.

He took a step toward Deacon as the movie went to black-and-white snow before replaying on a loop. "Why did you keep that recording all these years? And why play it now?" He intentionally positioned himself to give Marcia the most cover, moving another step forward to hold Deacon's attention.

The rifle pointed straight at him. Deacon held it at hip level, both hands keeping it steady. "Not another step, Max. I just did you a favor. I saved your life out there."

"You did. And for that I'm grateful. But I'm not so sure you intend for me to live out the rest of this evening. Otherwise you wouldn't have played that movie."

"Well, yes. There is that. I might have lied just a bit about not wanting to hurt either of you," he conceded in a companionable voice. "It's been so hard keeping that secret all these years when all I ever wanted to do was brag to anyone who would listen that I'd finally erased that scumbag from the Earth. He was sick. I could tell you stories for days about the things he did. But it didn't matter. Not to our father. He knew how evil Bobby was. But he was the firstborn, the heir. So Daddy dearest did nothing, turned the other way. The only concession to Bobby's sick tendencies was that Dad hired all those security thugs to keep an eye on him. Not that they did much good. Bobby had his hands in Daddy's money already and he used it to grease the palms of the guys who worked for our father. Soon they were his cohorts, covering his tracks instead of stopping him. You know that better than anyone, Max. They must have beaten you up half a dozen times while you were trying to get Bobby to back off from Bex. You should be thanking me for killing him."

"I repeat, why save the recording?" Max asked.

"For Bex, of course. I like Bex. She was always good to me back in school, even in middle school when I got teased and picked on so much, before I grew bigger and taller than the bullies and they became afraid of me. Before all that, Bex would take up for me, tell the bullies to leave me alone. Don't you remember the early years of middle school when the girls were taller than us, before we sprouted up? I do. Bex saved me from a lot of beatings back in the day. And I always regretted that I couldn't do more for her. Until Bobby. When I finally realized what he was doing, I vowed to figure out how to stop him once and for all. So I did. I saved Bex. And I cleaned up all the evidence of her having been there so your boss couldn't prosecute."

Max took another step toward Deacon, then stopped when the rifle raised to chest level. He put his hands in the air and wondered if Marcia was close enough to the door yet to make a run for it. "Easy, Deacon. I'm just trying to understand here. You saved Bex by killing Bobby, but then you let everyone think she was the one who killed him. Why?"

Deacon winced. "I hated that part. Of course,

I didn't want to go to prison. But I would have, if I had to. I saved that recording, and all of the evidence I took from the cabin, to use one day if I absolutely had to in order to keep her from being convicted. I would have sacrificed myself for her if it was necessary. You have to believe that. It's the only reason I saved such damning evidence."

He didn't know what to believe. But he played along. Why hadn't Marcia gone outside yet?

"I believe you," Max lied. "You were a good friend to Bex."

"Yes. I was."

"So what happens now?"

Deacon sighed. "Sadly, you and Marcia have to die. Neither of you will let Bobby's murder go. Ever since Bex came back to town, you've started digging, digging, digging. That has to stop. With you and Marcia gone, and my dad dying soon from the cancer, there won't be anyone left who cares enough to push for answers about Bobby's death."

Deacon's finger moved from the frame of the rifle to the trigger.

Max tried to stall him a little longer, inching closer. "Wait. I don't understand why you hired those gunmen—to grab Bex at the Piggly Wiggly? Or to scare her?"

Deacon shook his head. "Don't ask me. That was all dear old Dad's doing. Say a quick prayer,

Max. Renounce your sins. Because you're about to meet your maker."

"What about the blood?" Max rushed to ask him, holding his hands in the air. "If killing me is supposed to make the investigation into Bobby's death go away, won't my blood all over your living room just start a new investigation and put you right back in the same situation?"

"Well, I do plan on cleaning up the mess," Deacon reasoned.

"You can't clean up blood completely, not good enough so that a CSI guy can't find traces of it. You need to kill me outside, in the rain."

Deacon moved his finger back to the frame of the gun. "I know you're just stalling for time. But you do have a point. I wasn't too worried about blood when Bobby died, since it was all his anyway. But you're right. Explaining your DNA in my home might prove to be a problem. Move." He motioned with the rifle toward the front door.

The French door behind Max finally swung open, slamming back against the wall in a burst of wind and rain.

Deacon's eyes widened and he stepped to the right, swinging the rifle toward the door.

Max lunged toward him, praying he was close enough to reach him as Deacon swung the rifle back toward him.

Bam!

Chapter Twenty-One

Bex froze, her sneakers squishing in the mud just outside the cabin that had haunted her nightmares for over a decade. She raised the butcher knife that she'd grabbed from Max's kitchen and turned in a full circle. Was that a gunshot she'd heard? Or had the lightning hit one of the trees close by?

Rain pelted her from above, no longer blowing in stinging sheets. The storm was easing, but she was still soaked and cringing every time lightning flashed across the sky. She started forward again, using the flashlight she'd discovered in a kitchen drawer. Too bad Max hadn't had a gun in the kitchen drawer, too. She could have searched his house for one. But she'd been too worried the rain would obliterate his trail and she wouldn't be able to find him if she waited any longer.

Twenty minutes later, her pathetic tracking skills that she'd learned as a Girl Scout too many years ago to count had brought her to this cabin.

She shined the flashlight all around, hoping to see some sign of Max. She'd called his name over and over when she'd first started looking for him. But her voice was so hoarse now she didn't think she could scream if her life depended on it.

After testing the cabin's doorknob and finding it unlocked, she pushed it open, shining the light inside and holding her knife at the ready. But the one-room structure was obviously empty, and drenched and dirty from rain pelting through a hole in the roof. She whirled around and headed back to where she'd last seen a shoe print in the mud. Rain had already filled the print and was distorting its edges. She ran the light along the ground, weaving back and forth, searching for the next print. Nothing. Rain was running along the ground like a stream past the cabin, obliterating everything in its path.

She ran behind the cabin, shining her light all around. And then she saw it—another shoe print, heading toward the woods. Was it Max's? It seemed large enough to be but it was hard to tell. Not seeing any other prints nearby, and completely out of options, she started toward the trees.

MAX SLAMMED HIS FIST against Deacon's jaw. Deacon grunted in pain and rolled to the side. Max scrambled across the hardwood floor, reaching for the rifle that he'd knocked out of Deacon's hand earlier. Fingers circled around his ankle and yanked him backward.

He kicked his legs, slamming his boot into the side of Deacon's shoulder. Deacon let out a howl of pain and immediately let him go.

Max pushed himself up on his hands and knees and lunged for the rifle. He grabbed it, twisting around and bringing it up toward Deacon.

Except that Deacon was gone.

The sound of boots clomping across the porch outside the open French door had Max shoving to his feet and racing for the opening.

BEX HAD LOST the trail twenty feet from the cabin. But then she'd spotted a new trail, a recent trail. The pounding rain had distorted the prints so badly she could barely tell they were made by a human. But since any humans out in this storm had to either be Max or someone who could hopefully lead her to Max, she took off in pursuit. Jogging, head down, flashlight pointed at the ground so she wouldn't miss any of the rapidly disappearing prints, she hurried up an incline, faster and faster.

Wait. Incline? Weren't there cliffs around this area? She lifted her head and sucked in a breath at the black maw opening just ahead. She scrambled to stop her forward momentum, dropping to her knees in the mud at the cliff's edge. The knife flew out of her hands and disappeared over the side. Her feet slid in the muck, her momentum continuing to carry her toward the drop-off.

"Bex!"

She glanced over her shoulder to see Max running toward her. Her heart soared with relief that he was okay even as it swelled with panic as she slid toward the edge.

"Max!" She clawed desperately at the squishy ground.

He dived like a baseball player trying to steal first base, his hands outstretched. Her fingertips brushed against his, and then she fell into open air.

"BEX, NO!" MAX yelled her name, horrified, as her frightened, pale face disappeared over the cliff. He shoved to his knees, trying to find purchase in the slick mud. Digging his fingers around some tree roots embedded in the mire, he pulled himself just over the drop-off and looked down. "Bex? Bex?"

"I'm here."

Her voice sounded impossibly hoarse, but it was definitely her. He inched another half foot forward, and then he saw her, clinging to the side of the hill, the fingers of her left hand wrapped around tree roots protruding from the slick dirt.

"Hang on," he called down. "Don't let go."

"I'm slipping."

"Try to find a better handhold. There are roots all over the place. You might have to dig."

She punched at the dirt with her right hand. "I've got another root!"

"Good. Hold on. I'm coming to get you." How, he had no idea. But going over the edge wasn't an option. He'd pull the whole slick hillside down on top of both of them. He needed to go back down the hill and come up from beneath her, below the cliff face.

He half slid, half ran down the hill to circle around beneath the cliff. A shadow moved off to his right. He jerked his head around just as Deacon Caldwell slammed into him from the cover of trees.

Bex's left foot slid off her foothold and cartwheeled her sideways. She let out a squeal of alarm and scrabbled for a new foothold. The root she was holding in her right hand started to move. It was pulling loose. Where was Max?

A muffled grunt was her answer. The sound of cursing, a shout. Max was in trouble. Whoever was after him must have found him again. What in the world was happening?

"Bexley, look up."

She did, and was shocked to see Marcia Knolls's face pale in the moonlight, looking over the edge at her. Bex was even more surprised to see a rope being lowered. The rope stopped at her waist. All she had to do was grab it. In theory. But this was Marcia, the same woman who'd hated Bex all her life. The same woman who'd shot a bullet through her car window just a few days ago.

"Grab it," Marcia yelled. "What are you, stupid? You're going to fall."

The root suddenly pulled free, and Bex automatically grabbed for the rope. To her relief, it held. She looked up at Marcia, who had both hands wrapped around the rope above.

"It's tied around my waist," she said. "I'm a lot bigger than you, and stronger. But you're still going to have to help. Try to climb up while I pull."

Bex slammed the toe of her sneaker against the wall of dirt until she made a deep enough gap to get a toehold. She tried to think of it like climbing a rock wall for exercise, only without the steep drop to almost-certain death below. Inch by inch, working as a team, she and Marcia managed to pull her all the way to the edge.

But Marcia didn't move to help her climb up.

"Marcia," Bex gasped. "Move back. I can't climb up with you right in front of me."

A slow, feral smile curved Marcia's lips. "I know. And the end of the rope isn't tied around my waist, either. All that's keeping you from falling to your death are two loops of rope around my wrist. Kind of makes you wish you were nicer to me in high school, doesn't it? Or that you'd kept your hands off my freaking boyfriend."

Bex stared at her in horror, seeing her own death mirrored in the other woman's black eyes.

MAX GRAPPLED IN the mud with Deacon, both of them fighting for control of the rifle. Sirens sounded in the distance, drawing ever closer.

Deacon's mouth contorted with rage. "Damn my father. He must have heard the gunshot and called the cops."

"Just let the gun go," Max gasped, straining against the man who outweighed him by a good thirty pounds, most of it muscle. "No one else has to get hurt." He wrenched one hand free and slammed it under Deacon's jaw.

Deacon fell back against the ground, cursing. Both men lost their grip on the gun. It went flying over their heads, landing somewhere near the tree line. Deacon got to his feet first, shoving himself toward the woods. Max punched him in the middle of his spine. A bloodcurdling scream filled the air and Deacon flipped onto his back, arching off the ground and whimpering like a dog that had been kicked in the ribs.

Max whirled around and sprinted toward the

cliff to find Bex. His stomach clenched with dread when he saw Marcia on her knees at the edge, a rope wrapped around her left hand. Just beyond her, Bex clutched the other end of the rope with one hand, while clawing at the dirt with her other hand, desperately seeking a handhold.

The sirens stopped somewhere down the hill, back toward the cabin. But Max couldn't wait for backup. He slipped and slid on the muddy ground, using both his hands and his feet to make his way toward Marcia and Bex. Then moonlight reflected off what was lying on the ground beside Marcia.

A machete.

Shouts sounded from farther down the incline. Blue and red lights flashed. Deacon was coming after him. But Max couldn't waste even a second to turn around.

He half ran, half slid the last few yards toward Bex, watching with horror as Marcia raised the machete.

"No!" Max dived forward in a rolling slide, grabbing Bex's arms. He swung her up and over the cliff toward solid ground as the machete arced through the air.

Wind rushed beside Max and Bex as the wicked blade narrowly missed both of them. But without something to block her forward momentum, Marcia couldn't stop herself. She screamed as she plummeted over the side of the cliff. Then her scream was abruptly cut off.

Bex cried out in horror. "No, Marcia!"

They both carefully looked over the edge. Bex cried out again and closed her eyes.

Max pulled her to him, rocking her against his chest. "There was nothing we could do."

A guttural shout of rage sounded from down the hill. Max jerked his head around just as near the tree line Deacon brought up his rifle, swinging it toward them.

Max shoved Bex to the ground, covering her body with his as the rifle boomed.

Everything went silent.

Even the thunder had stopped, and the rain had slowed to a gentle mist.

Max slowly lifted his head.

Deacon Caldwell lay in the mud twenty feet away, his sightless eyes staring up at the moon overhead. And behind him, standing with the aid of a cane, was his father. Holding a pistol. He stared a long moment at Max and Bex. Then his shoulders slumped and he slowly lowered the gun. Without a word, he dropped it in the mud and started hobbling back down the slope.

Bex pushed herself up on her elbows, her eyes wide and frightened. "What just happened?"

"Deacon's father saved our lives. I have no idea why."

She blinked as if she couldn't comprehend what he was saying. And then she covered her face with her hands and collapsed against him, great gasping sobs making her entire body shake.

"Ah, honey." Max scooped her up in his arms and rocked her against him.

The hillside erupted into chaos. Max's SWAT team descended upon them, securing the scene. Thornton started barking out orders. And soon a team of EMTs was racing up the hill.

Max didn't wait for them. He ran with his precious burden to a waiting ambulance.

Chapter Twenty-Two

Two months later...

Bex stood at the wall of glass, watching the season's first snowfall drift down onto Max's deck. This was her first day back in Destiny since she'd nearly fallen to her death off a cliff and Max was almost killed by the one Caldwell who'd ever shown Bex a kernel of kindness. She was still trying to come to terms with everything that had happened. But it was going to take a while.

Strong, warm arms wrapped around her waist and pulled her back against a solid, familiar chest. She wrapped her arms over Max's and sighed.

"I love you," she said.

"I know. You don't have to keep telling me that. I'm convinced."

"And?"

"And I love you, too." His voice was husky and deep with emotion.

She sighed again, happier than she'd ever thought she could be.

He kissed the side of her neck and gently swayed with her in his arms as they watched fall turn into winter right before their eyes.

"I never heard what happened to the cashier who helped that gang at the Piggly Wiggly," she said. "Reggie, right?"

"Thornton argued for her to be sent to a minimum security facility instead of doing hard time. She's finally getting the counseling she needs. Maybe without her ex-con father's influence, she'll turn her life around and not end up like him."

"That was awfully nice of your boss."

"He's not the ogre you think he is."

She shrugged, not quite ready to forgive. Although she was pretty sure she would one day soon.

"Is everything finally settled with Robert Caldwell Senior?" she asked.

"Mmm-hmm. He confessed to hiring the gunmen. He was convinced you'd killed his son. But after hearing the gunshot the night we were on the cliff, and driving out to his son's house and seeing that recording, he couldn't fool himself any longer. I guess we owe our lives to the fact that Deacon kept that recording. If his father hadn't seen it before tracking us, he might not have chosen to shoot Deacon. He'd probably have shot us."

She shivered, the memories of that night still capable of giving her nightmares. "What happens to Mr. Caldwell now?"

"Nothing. He's under hospice care. He probably won't live out the week. And I don't know about you, but I think he's suffered enough for his sins. Losing two sons, one by his own hand, has to be devastating."

"You feel sorry for him?"

"I suppose I do."

She squeezed his arms. "I'm not surprised. You're a good man. You care about people, whether they deserve it or not."

"If that's yet another way of apologizing or saying you aren't worthy of my love, knock it off."

He knew her so well. She turned her head to the side and rubbed her cheek against his chest. He rested his head on top of hers and they stood there a long time, content just to hold each other.

Finally, he said, "How did your assistant, Allison, take the news that you're taking an extended leave of absence from the antique shop to spend some time with me?"

She stiffened in his arms. "That's not exactly what I told her."

He stepped back and turned her around to

face him. His brows were a dark slash of worry. "You've changed your mind?"

"I guess you could say that. I sold my store to her."

He couldn't have looked more surprised. "But I thought you loved restoring and selling antiques."

"I do. But I can do that anywhere. Like, say, in Destiny."

He grew very still, his eyes blazing at her with an intensity that had her whole body flushing hot.

"What are you saying, Bex?"

She slid her arms around his waist and tilted her head back to look at him. "I'm saying that with Bobby Caldwell's case finally closed, and nothing else hanging over my head, it's time that I rectified a terrible decision I made many years ago."

His throat worked, but no sound came out.

She cleared her own throat, already getting tight with emotion. "Max, I love you so much. I was wondering…"

"Yes?" he rasped.

"I was wondering if I could wear one of your T-shirts."

He blinked, then threw his head back and laughed, a great booming sound that filled her heart with joy. He grinned and scooped her up in his arms, then jogged through the house to his bedroom. He didn't stop until he was in front of the chest of drawers. Then he settled her against him, holding her with one arm as he yanked the top drawer open.

"Any particular T-shirt you prefer, Bexley Kane?"

She dipped her hand into the drawer and pulled out the black velvet box. "This one will do nicely."

He turned serious, cradling her against him as if he'd never let her go. His eyes darkened with more love than seemed possible for one person to hold in his heart for another. More love than Bex could ever hope to deserve. But she would happily spend the rest of her life trying, and loving him back even more.

"And I prefer to be called Mrs. Remington from this day forward, if you don't mind."

His mouth slowly lowered to hers, stopping inches away as he carried her toward the bed. "I don't mind, Mrs. Remington. I don't mind at all." And then he kissed her.

* * * * *

Look for more books in award-winning author
Lena Diaz's miniseries
TENNESSEE SWAT, *coming soon.*

You'll find them wherever
Harlequin Intrigue books are sold!

LARGER-PRINT BOOKS!

HARLEQUIN *Presents*

GET 2 FREE LARGER-PRINT NOVELS PLUS 2 FREE GIFTS!

YES! Please send me 2 FREE LARGER-PRINT Harlequin Presents® novels and my 2 FREE gifts (gifts are worth about $10). After receiving them, if I don't wish to receive any more books, I can return the shipping statement marked "cancel." If I don't cancel, I will receive 6 brand-new novels every month and be billed just $5.30 per book in the U.S. or $5.74 per book in Canada. That's a saving of at least 12% off the cover price! It's quite a bargain! Shipping and handling is just 50¢ per book in the U.S. and 75¢ per book in Canada.* I understand that accepting the 2 free books and gifts places me under no obligation to buy anything. I can always return a shipment and cancel at any time. Even if I never buy another book, the two free books and gifts are mine to keep forever.

176/376 HDN GHVY

Name _____ (PLEASE PRINT)

Address _____ Apt. #

City _____ State/Prov. _____ Zip/Postal Code

Signature (if under 18, a parent or guardian must sign)

Mail to the Reader Service:
IN U.S.A.: P.O. Box 1867, Buffalo, NY 14240-1867
IN CANADA: P.O. Box 609, Fort Erie, Ontario L2A 5X3

Are you a subscriber to Harlequin Presents® books and want to receive the larger-print edition? Call 1-800-873-8635 today or visit us at www.ReaderService.com.

* Terms and prices subject to change without notice. Prices do not include applicable taxes. Sales tax applicable in N.Y. Canadian residents will be charged applicable taxes. Offer not valid in Quebec. This offer is limited to one order per household. Not valid for current subscribers to Harlequin Presents Larger-Print books. All orders subject to credit approval. Credit or debit balances in a customer's account(s) may be offset by any other outstanding balance owed by or to the customer. Please allow 4 to 6 weeks for delivery. Offer available while quantities last.

Your Privacy—The Reader Service is committed to protecting your privacy. Our Privacy Policy is available online at www.ReaderService.com or upon request from the Reader Service.

We make a portion of our mailing list available to reputable third parties that offer products we believe may interest you. If you prefer that we not exchange your name with third parties, or if you wish to clarify or modify your communication preferences, please visit us at www.ReaderService.com/consumerchoice or write to us at Reader Service Preference Service, P.O. Box 9062, Buffalo, NY 14240-9062. Include your complete name and address.

HPLP15

LARGER-PRINT BOOKS!

GET 2 FREE LARGER-PRINT NOVELS PLUS
2 FREE GIFTS!

⊕ HARLEQUIN®

Romance

From the Heart, For the Heart

YES! Please send me 2 FREE LARGER-PRINT Harlequin® Romance novels and my 2 FREE gifts (gifts are worth about $10). After receiving them, if I don't wish to receive any more books, I can return the shipping statement marked "cancel." If I don't cancel, I will receive 4 brand-new novels every month and be billed just $5.09 per book in the U.S. or $5.49 per book in Canada. That's a savings of at least 15% off the cover price! It's quite a bargain! Shipping and handling is just 50¢ per book in the U.S. and 75¢ per book in Canada.* I understand that accepting the 2 free books and gifts places me under no obligation to buy anything. I can always return a shipment and cancel at any time. Even if I never buy another book, the two free books and gifts are mine to keep forever.

119/319 HDN GHWC

Name	(PLEASE PRINT)

Address	Apt. #

City	State/Prov.	Zip/Postal Code

Signature (if under 18, a parent or guardian must sign)

Mail to the **Reader Service:**
IN U.S.A.: P.O. Box 1867, Buffalo, NY 14240-1867
IN CANADA: P.O. Box 609, Fort Erie, Ontario L2A 5X3

Want to try two free books from another line?
Call 1-800-873-8635 or visit www.ReaderService.com.

* Terms and prices subject to change without notice. Prices do not include applicable taxes. Sales tax applicable in N.Y. Canadian residents will be charged applicable taxes. Offer not valid in Quebec. This offer is limited to one order per household. Not valid for current subscribers to Harlequin Romance Larger-Print books. All orders subject to credit approval. Credit or debit balances in a customer's account(s) may be offset by any other outstanding balance owed by or to the customer. Please allow 4 to 6 weeks for delivery. Offer available while quantities last.

Your Privacy—The Reader Service is committed to protecting your privacy. Our Privacy Policy is available online at www.ReaderService.com or upon request from the Reader Service.

We make a portion of our mailing list available to reputable third parties that offer products we believe may interest you. If you prefer that we not exchange your name with third parties, or if you wish to clarify or modify your communication preferences, please visit us at www.ReaderService.com/consumerschoice or write to us at Reader Service Preference Service, P.O. Box 9062, Buffalo, NY 14240-9062. Include your complete name and address.

HRLP15